P9-DGN-379

CHRISTMAS CALAMITY AT THE VICARAGE

A Churchill & Pemberley Novella

EMILY ORGAN

Copyright © 2019 by Emily Organ
This edition copyright © 2022
All rights reserved.

emilyorgan.com

Emily Organ has asserted her right under the Copyright, Designs and
Patents Act 1988 to be identified as the author of this work.

All characters and events in this publication, other than those clearly in
the public domain, are fictitious and any resemblance to real persons,
living or dead, is purely coincidental.

ISBN 978-1-9993433-8-5

This book is copyright material and must not be copied, reproduced,
transferred, distributed, leased, licensed or publicly performed or used
in any way except as specifically permitted in writing by the publisher, as
allowed under the terms and conditions under which it was purchased
or as strictly permitted by applicable copyright law. Any unauthorised
distribution or use of this text may be a direct infringement of the
author's and publisher's rights and those responsible may be liable in
law accordingly.

Christmas Calamity at the Vicarage

Emily Organ

~

Books in the Churchill & Pemberley Series:

Chapter One

"It's almost Christmas!" chimed Annabel Churchill as she hung cheerful red and silver baubles on the little fir tree in her office. "Good tidings of great joy and all that lark. I do like Christmas. Do you like Christmas, Pembers?"

"I think it's wonderful," replied her secretary Doris Pemberley, who was sitting at her desk with a scruffy dog on her lap.

"I'm so glad."

"Oswald *adores* Christmas." Pemberley patted the dog's head affectionately.

"How do you know that? This is the first Christmas you'll have spent with him."

"I can just tell that he does."

"That's lovely. How is the festive season usually celebrated here in Compton Poppleford? What's the main event?"

"It's all about the Vicarage Christmas Party."

"Is it any good?"

"Most of the villagers attend."

"But is it any good?"

"The vicar provides sherry and bitters."

"I like the sound of those."

"And a mince pie mountain."

"That's clinched it! When is this fine event to be held?"

"It's usually the Saturday before Christmas Day unless that day is Christmas Eve, in which case it's the Saturday before it."

"Which is?"

"This Saturday."

"Well, I'm game if you are, Pembers. Shall we attend the special soirée together?"

"Of course. Can Oswald come?"

"I don't see why not. Does the vicar like dogs?"

"He loves them."

"Perfect."

Pemberley gave an excited gasp. "I just saw a snowflake float past the window!"

"Really?" Churchill dashed over to Pemberley's desk and peered out. "Oh yes! Look at that!"

A light dusting of snow was beginning to collect on the rooftops along the high street, and Churchill felt a skip of joy beneath her large bosom.

"No matter how old one is, a bit of snow always lifts the spirits, doesn't it?" she exclaimed.

The two ladies quietly watched the snow falling for a moment or two.

"How will you be spending this Christmas, Mrs Churchill?"

"I shall return to my former haunt of Richmond-upon-Thames for a Christmas lunch with my old acquaintances."

"The ladies from the Richmond-upon-Thames Ladies' Lawn Tennis Club, you mean?"

"Some of them, yes. What about you, Pembers?"

"I usually spend Christmas with my nephew and his wife in Burton Bradstock."

"How lovely."

"But I can't go this year."

"Why not?"

"Because I'd like Oswald to spend his first Christmas at home."

"Just you and Oswald on Christmas Day?"

"Yes. What's wrong with that?"

"Won't you get bored?"

"How could I possibly be bored when Oswald is around?"

"I suppose it would be a little more interesting if he could play backgammon."

"I adore backgammon."

"Do you really, Pembers? I didn't realise that. So do I."

"If you weren't heading off to Richmond-upon-Thames for Christmas we could have played it."

"Perhaps we could do so on my return. We have the Vicarage Christmas Party to look forward to in the meantime. A mince pie mountain, eh? I had no idea Christmas in Compton Poppleford would be so exciting."

Chapter Two

THE SNOW WAS FALLING thick and heavy as the two ladies and dog approached Compton Poppleford vicarage a few days later. The early evening light was fading fast and bright lights glimmered from the windows.

"It's chilly tonight," commented Pemberley.

"You need a thicker coat," replied Churchill. "There isn't enough meat on your bones for this sort of weather. I, on the other hand, find myself naturally blessed with a little extra coverage."

"A drop of sherry will warm me up."

"I'm sure it will. That mince pie mountain will help as well, Pembers. I feel quite certain it'll cure me of all my ills."

"You can't eat the entire mountain single-handedly, Mrs Churchill."

"No, of course not! Just a little nibble of the summit will suit me." Churchill felt her mouth watering at the thought of the crisp, buttery pastry and the rich, sweet fruit. "In fact, I shall probably spend the duration of the party in the company of the mince pie mountain. There won't be a great deal else to do, will there?"

"The choir will be singing Christmas carols."

"I'll be able to hear them from my position beside the mince pies, no doubt."

"And Mr Hurricks will be reading from Charles Dickens's *A Christmas Carol*."

"We're all rather au fait with that story, aren't we? I shan't be missing out on much there."

"You won't want to forgo a game of Pass the Pudding."

"I almost certainly will."

"No, you won't. Pass the Pudding is a village tradition!"

"There are plenty of traditions in this village that I'm more than happy to leave well alone, Pembers."

"But you absolutely must play Pass the Pudding."

"What does it involve?"

"Mrs Robertson steams the pudding in November, then wraps it in muslin."

"That doesn't sound like much of a game."

"No, that's just the making of the pudding."

"And the game itself?"

"The pudding is brought to the vicarage in great ceremony by Father Christmas, and must then be passed along the line of party guests without anyone using their hands."

"Oh no! Not *that* sort of game."

"What's wrong with that?"

"It gives people the excuse to become a little frisky, if you catch my drift."

"I've never known anyone become particularly frisky while playing it."

"Perhaps everyone is better behaved here in Dorset than in Richmond-upon-Thames, then."

$\sim$

"*Deck the halls with boughs of holly!*" sang a host of cheerful voices from just beyond the entrance to the vicarage. Churchill admired the wreath of holly and mistletoe as she rattled the brass knocker.

"Christmas has truly arrived, hasn't it, Pembers? What a lovely sound, and what a wonderful garland on the door here."

"*'Tis the season to be jolly!*" chorused the choir as the door swung open and the two old ladies stepped into the hallway.

Churchill felt a glow of warmth as she took in the joyful singers beside the Christmas tree, which glittered with little candles and decorations. A pleasing scent of cinnamon and nutmeg hung in the air, and an apple-cheeked maid beamed at the two ladies as she took their coats. Then she glanced down and scowled.

"Oh, that pesky dog's back again. I'll shoo 'im out."

"No, please don't!" protested Pemberley. "It's Oswald!"

"Got a name, 'as 'e? Well, it ain't gonna stop 'im being a naughty little so an' so."

"He's my dog," replied Pemberley, "and we've brought him here with us."

"Your dog, is 'e? I thought 'e were a stray."

"No, he belongs to me."

"Well, 'e spends a lotta time runnin' round the village causin' trouble, 'e does."

"He's only escaped once or twice," retorted Churchill. "You must be confusing him with someone else."

"Some*dog* else," corrected Pemberley.

"Let's find you a sherry, Pembers."

The two ladies walked on through the vicarage, greeting familiar faces as they went. Churchill was surprised by the size of the place. Room after room appeared to be filled with chattering guests. The sherry and bitters were laid out on a table in the library.

"Oh, I do like the look of all the books in here," said Pemberley, perusing the shelves. "How I'd love to sit down and read them all!"

"Some people are blessed with plenty of time to do so," replied Churchill, placing her handbag on the table and examining a decanter of sherry. "I never find enough hours in the day myself. Books are rather long, aren't they? Especially *Wuthering Heights*. That took me forever to plough through."

Nearby, the vicar was conversing with a bearded man wearing a waistcoat that was too small to be buttoned around his expansive midriff.

"Ah, Mrs Churchill! Miss Pemberley!" crowed the vicar, a tall, large-nosed man with thin wisps of hair and watery grey eyes. "How lovely to see you. I do believe this is your first Vicarage Christmas Party, Mrs Churchill. Am I right?"

"You are indeed, Vicar. And I've heard tell of a mince pie mountain."

"Oh dear, let me fetch someone to shoo that dog out," he said, glaring down at Oswald.

"Please don't, he belongs to me!" Pemberley piped up.

"Does he really? But that's the little dog who always seems to be causing trouble around here."

"Not at all. He's rarely out of my sight, actually. You must be thinking of somedog else."

"Is that so? He looks remarkably similar to the dog who stole our sausages last week. Cook only opened the door for a couple of minutes!"

"That definitely sounds like another dog," replied Churchill, adding a dash of Angostura bitters to her sherry.

The large bearded man gave a hearty laugh, which instantly made Oswald overexcited.

"He looks like a fine fellow to me!" the man bellowed as he stooped to pet the dog. "What is he? A mongrel?"

"He's a Spanish water dog," said Pemberley, "with a bit of spaniel and terrier mixed in."

"Well, well, well. What a delightful combination!" He bent his head down and the little dog enthusiastically licked his face.

The vicar winkled his nose. "I believe you already know Mr Hurricks, Miss Pemberley. Mrs Churchill, this is Mr Hurricks, head of the Compton Poppleford Amateur Dramatics Society."

"It's a pleasure to meet you, Mrs Churchill!" replied Mr Hurricks, cackling as he rose to full height again.

"Likewise, and most delighted, I'm sure," replied Churchill.

The vicar became distracted by Oswald sniffing his foot. "Does he bite?" he ventured nervously.

"He's never bitten anyone in his life," replied Pemberley.

"Ouch!" The vicar recoiled in pain.

"What happened?" Pemberley bent down and scooped the dog up.

"He just bit my ankle!" wailed the vicar, hopping on one foot.

Mr Hurricks guffawed.

"I'm terribly sorry," said Pemberley. "Is there any blood?"

The vicar stopped hopping and bent down to pull up his trouser leg. He unhooked the sock suspender and rolled down his sock.

"No," he whimpered, closely examining his ankle, "but he's broken the skin."

"Naughty, Oswald!" scolded Pemberley. "You mustn't break the vicar's skin!"

"Shall we call for assistance, Vicar?" asked Churchill. "No doubt there's a doctor here this evening."

"Dr Bratchett's here, but there's no need to call him. I shall be quite all right, thank you." He refastened his sock and lowered his trouser leg.

"Nothing too serious, eh, Vicar?" said Mr Hurricks. "I should think you'll live to see Christmas Day."

"Let's go and find the mince pies, Miss Pemberley," suggested Churchill.

~

The two ladies left the library and made their way into the wood-panelled dining room, where more sherry and bitters were laid out on the table.

"You should have left that dog at home, Pembers," scolded Churchill.

"Leave him alone at Christmastime? Never!"

"You're lucky he didn't cause the vicar any lasting damage."

"It was only a playful nip. He wasn't even bleeding!"

"You and I can endure playful nips without issue, Pembers, but some people are a little more sensitive."

"A little too sensitive, I should say."

"We're all different, and that's what makes the world such an interesting place. Now, where is this mince pie mountain? I must speak honestly, Pembers, and confess that it's the only reason I turned up."

"I'm not sure where they've put it," replied Pemberley, glancing around.

"Oh, hello Mrs Churchill and Miss Pemberley!" A jolly lady in a red tea dress that matched the colour of her hair approached. "And Oswald, too! You're all here at the Vicarage Christmas Party!"

"We are indeed, Mrs Thonnings," replied Churchill. "Well observed. You don't happen to know the location of the mince pie mountain, do you?"

"No, I haven't seen it. I expect you're both enjoying a well-earned break from sleuthing, am I right?"

"We are indeed," said Churchill absently as she looked around for signs of the festive pastry. Disappointingly, none of the other guests appeared to be eating or holding a mince pie. "Perhaps it's already gone," she added sadly.

"What's gone?" asked Mrs Thonnings.

"The mince pie mountain. Perhaps it's already been eaten."

"I didn't get a chance to eat any either, if it has. I think I saw Mr Hurricks with two mince pies earlier."

Churchill sighed. "It wouldn't surprise me if he'd consumed most of the mountain himself, judging by the man's size. Quite selfish, really, when it's the time of year to be thinking of one's fellow man or woman."

"Perhaps I'm mistaken and some of the mountain is still intact," said Mrs Thonnings. "I haven't been in all the rooms yet." She drained her sherry. "Are you working on any interesting cases at the moment? I'm so fascinated by your work. Oh, how I wish I had a few cases myself!"

"As I've explained to you a number of times, Mrs Thonnings, there is nothing particularly fascinating about our cases."

"Nothing fascinating about solving murders?"

"Solving murders accounts for only a small part of our work, and even that can be rather tedious work at times."

"Why do you do it, then?"

"Well, one enjoys the challenge."

"I would enjoy the challenge, too! What do you need help with at the moment?"

"Nothing in particular, Mrs Thonnings. Miss Pemberley and I are taking a break from our work over Christmas."

"Oh no! Are we really?" protested her secretary.

"Yes. It's important to have a little breather from all the busy days, Miss Pemberley."

"But I don't want a breather. I enjoy our work!"

"There you go, you see!" added Mrs Thonnings. "Miss Pemberley enjoys the work so much that she doesn't want to take a break. Not even at Christmastime!"

"Well, that's Miss Pemberley for you. Besides, we can only work when there is work to be done. Nobody needs any cases solving at Christmastime, do they?"

Chapter Three

"WHERE ELSE CAN we look for this elusive mountain of mince pies?" asked Churchill. "Do you really think Mr Hurricks might have eaten the lot, Pembers? I wouldn't put it past him, you know. People of a certain size can't be trusted around such delicious edible goods. And I speak as someone who knows about these things."

They were just stepping out of the dining room to continue their search when a bell tinkled.

"Please make your way to the drawing room for a performance by the Compton Poppleford Choir!" rang out the vicar's voice.

"It's rather difficult to listen attentively to a choir when one's stomach is rumbling, don't you think, Pembers?"

~

A Christmas tree stood at the far end of the drawing room, and before it were arranged the twenty or so members of the choir, whose ages ranged from five to ninety-five. Once everyone was squashed into the room the vicar stood in front of the choir and welcomed his guests.

"This is the thirty-second Vicarage Christmas Party that I have personally hosted here, and every Christmas I am more than delighted with the turnout from this parish. I would like to remind you all of the busy schedule we have in the church at this time of year."

Churchill's stomach gave another rumble. Oswald sat by her feet and scratched his ear as the vicar rattled off a long list of Christmas church services. He eventually introduced Mr Donkin the choirmaster and a smattering of applause followed.

Mr Donkin was a jolly, red-faced man who greeted his audience with a wide smile and a perfunctory bow. He wore a colourful cravat with a festive holly-leaf design and a matching waistcoat. To Churchill's chagrin, he held a half-eaten mince pie in one hand, which he summarily polished off before addressing the crowd.

"Thank you, ladies and gentlemen! Thank you very much indeed! On behalf of the Compton Poppleford Choir, may I express how delighted we are to be performing for you all this evening. You may already have heard us in the entrance hall as you arrived, but I ask you to listen again as we sing, for your delight, our most favourite Christmas carols. And now, without further ado, may I introduce to you the wonderful... the delightful... the magnificent... Compton... Poppleford... Choir!"

He turned to face his group, and with a wave of the baton the choir promptly embarked on a rendition of several popular carols. Mr Donkin bounced and jiggled all the while as he conducted them.

Churchill's foot tapped in time as she enjoyed the familiar Christmas songs, but she couldn't help but glance around to ascertain where the choirmaster had obtained his mince pie from.

"I think some sort of hidden knowledge is required," she whispered to Pemberley.

"What for?"

"For the mince pies. I think one must have to seek them out somehow. They're not in an obvious spot, if you know what I mean. Perhaps their location is only revealed to the initiated."

"Why don't you ask Mr Donkin where he got his from?"

"Oh, I intend to, but I'll have to wait until he's stopped writhing around like a tadpole first. Must he move his hips like that to *God Rest Ye Merry Gentlemen*? It's bordering on the obscene."

Churchill was more than ready to seek out the evasive party food by the time the carols had finished.

"Thank goodness that's over, Pembers. I'm well and truly famished!"

The vicar took up his place in front of the choir once again and urged everyone to remain where they were. He held up a large envelope in one hand and an ornamental letter opener in the other.

"I shall now announce the winner of the Christmas cake competition," he announced. "May I take this opportunity to commend all those who took part for the high standard of entries this year. My cook, Mrs Robertson, and I thoroughly enjoyed sampling each and every one of them. In fact, we spent some extremely pleasant afternoons seated in my dining room with a pot of Earl Grey and an array of fruit cakes that had been baked to perfection. All those lovely plump fruits soaked in brandy, and such sweet, soft marzipan. Not to mention the wonderful sugary icing!"

Churchill gave an involuntary groan and Pemberley shot her a concerned glance.

"I'm almost done for, Pembers," she whispered. "There isn't a single scrap of food to be found at the vicar's party, and then he taunts us with tales of cake!"

"It's certainly not the right way to tend to his flock," replied Pemberley.

They listened as the vicar described each Christmas cake entry at length, and Churchill gave an audible sigh of relief when he finally inserted the tip of his dagger-shaped letter opener into the corner of the envelope, slicing it open in one smooth movement.

He removed a piece of paper from inside. "And the winner is…" He paused and scanned around the room to create even more suspense.

"Oh, get on with it," muttered Churchill.

"Mrs…"

The vicar's face broke out into a grin and he rolled his watery grey eyes in a jocular fashion.

Churchill's stomach gave another angst-ridden grumble. "I haven't been this hungry since someone stole my tuck box at Princess Alexandra's School for Young Ladies," she whispered.

"Mrs Stonecastle!" announced the vicar.

A round of applause erupted around the room and the vicar scanned the audience expectantly, waiting for Mrs Stonecastle to come forward.

"She's behind you!" someone called out.

"Oh, is she? Oh yes, of course she is. She's a member of the choir!"

A slight, demure-looking lady with brown curls stepped forward and gave the vicar a bashful smile.

"Mrs Stonecastle! I must heartily congratulate you on your most delightful Christmas cake!" exclaimed the vicar.

"What's the prize?" Churchill asked Pemberley.

"There is no prize; just the satisfaction of winning."

"At least we'll get to sample some of her prize-winning cake."

"I doubt it. The vicar and his staff usually eat it all."

Churchill gave a loud snort. "So much for distributing the spoils! The Bible must say something about sharing cake among the flock. Anyway, now that's all over we can resume our search for sustenance. Perhaps there's something tucked away in the parlour."

The choir began to file out of the room in an orderly fashion, and the two ladies were just about to follow behind them when the vicar made another announcement.

"Wait there, ladies and gentlemen. Don't go anywhere! Please take your seats and prepare yourselves for the next round of entertainment."

"Good grief, Pembers!" Churchill was beginning to feel weak at the knees. "What can it possibly be now?"

"Back again by popular demand," continued the vicar, "and I know that for many of you this is the absolute highlight of the Vicarage Christmas Party... Please welcome Mr Hurricks for his recital of Mr Charles Dickens's *A Christmas Carol*!"

Applause and cheers resounded around the room as Mr Hurricks's large frame took up position in front of the Christmas tree, book in hand.

"Heavens above! Does he intend to read the whole thing, Pembers?"

"I think it's slightly abridged."

"I'm in danger of becoming slightly abridged myself at this rate. Come on, let's leave with the choir."

"But we're not supposed to move. Mr Hurricks is just about to begin his performance."

"It's all right for him, though. He's already eaten two mince pies!"

The opening lines of *A Christmas Carol* boomed out across the room in a stentorian voice.

"Crikey! There's no doubt that he has the perfect vocal cords for the stage, is there? Come on, let's go before the door is closed on us."

"But we're not allowed to leave!"

"We'll tell the vicar that I'm feeling faint if he asks. And I can honestly say that it's close to the truth. Come along!"

~

As the two ladies stepped out of the room, Pemberley supported Churchill's arm in a bid to demonstrate to those gathered that she was in need of assistance. Oswald trotted along behind them.

"Here we are," said Pemberley, pausing outside the library. "You can have a seat in here, Mrs Churchill."

"But there's no food in here!"

"I thought you were feeling faint."

"I am, but only because I need to eat. Let's try the parlour, as I suggested earlier."

The two ladies continued on their way, with Mr Hurricks's theatrical voice floating after them from the drawing room.

"I think the food must be in the parlour, Pembers," said Churchill. "I can hear voices coming from that direction."

Feeling encouraged, they strode up to the door and saw that the Compton Poppleford Choir had almost filled the room.

Churchill was just about to express her grave concern that the choir had finished off any remaining food there might have been, when she realised they were all standing rather quietly and attentively. Holding the singers' attention with his back to the two ladies was Mr Donkin.

The choir members did not appear as jovial as they had during their performance; in fact, some of the children's faces were crumpled and close to tears. Mr Donkin was no longer dancing around, either. He was standing quite still, with one hand gripping his baton so tightly that his knuckles were white.

Chapter Four

"CALL THAT A PERFORMANCE?" snarled the choirmaster. "What on earth happened to the harmonies we practised for '*Ding Dong Merrily on High*'? You were so flat I could have nailed four legs to you and called you a table!"

Pemberley gave Churchill a baffled look.

"And that rendition of '*Jingle Bells*'," continued Mr Donkin, "was the most discordant wailing I've heard since three stray cats got trapped in the dustbin round the back of the Wagon and Carrot!"

"Poor cats!" whispered Pemberley.

The ticking off became too much for one little boy, who stood clasping a toy snowman in one hand. He burst into tears.

"Stop that pitiful snivelling, child!" scolded Mr Donkin, pointing his baton at the boy. "If you don't like what you're hearing, you may go ahead and leave. And take your tone-deaf mother with you!"

Churchill had heard enough. "That's no way to speak to your loyal choristers, Mr Donkin!" she called out.

He spun around in startled surprise.

"And at Christmas of all times!" she continued. "Where's your festive spirit?"

There was an uncomfortable silence as the choirmaster glowered at the two old ladies. Churchill's stomach gave another loud grumble.

"My *festive spirit* left me as soon as this lot opened their mouths and squawked out the first line of '*Silent Night*'!" fumed Mr Donkin.

"Well, I thought they sounded quite marvellous. Don't you agree, Miss Pemberley?"

"Yes. I thought everyone sang beautifully and I enjoyed it immensely. Everyone did."

"Quite so," said Churchill. "It seems you have built up unrealistic expectations of your choir, Mr Donkin, but bullying them in this manner will get you nowhere. In fact, you're lucky to have a choir at all if you're in the habit of speaking to them like that. I think they'd be better off leaving and finding themselves a new choirmaster."

"Hear, hear!" called out Mrs Stonecastle, still feeling flush from winning the Christmas cake competition.

Mr Donkin placed his hands on his hips and scowled. "Who are you, anyway? And what gives you the right to lecture me on how I manage my choir?"

"I'm Mrs Annabel Churchill, your local private detective, and this is my assistant, Miss Pemberley. I'm not lecturing you on how to manage your choir, Mr Donkin, I was merely suggesting that you speak to them a little more politely. Deliberately upsetting small boys is really quite unacceptable."

"I'll manage my choir in whatever way I see fit, thank you very much," retorted the choirmaster. "And I'd thank you two old, interfering busybodies to mind your own business."

"You mustn't speak to elderly ladies like that!" a man with wavy grey hair piped up. "Have you no respect, man? Your comments about '*Jingle Bells*' were partially justified, but for a chap to sink so low as to start hurling insults at old ladies... Well, I must say that I've had enough of this choir. I hear the one in Heythrop Itching is so much better, and now I'm not sure why I didn't just join that one in the first place."

"Hear, hear!" Mrs Stonecastle called out again as a general muttering struck up among the choir members.

"Silence!" shouted Mr Donkin, who was completely ignored. "Silence!" he shouted again, but again no one paid him any attention. He turned back to Churchill. "Do you see what you've done now? No one's listening to me! This is mutiny, this is!"

The choir began to disperse and several members pushed past him as they made their way out of the room.

"Where are you going?" he called after them. "We need to talk about rehearsals for the Christmas Eve carols in the marketplace!"

"Good luck with that, Bob," replied the man with the wavy hair. "At this rate you'll be doing it on your own."

"But I can't sing!"

"You should have thought about that before you went around upsetting us all."

"That's marvellous, that is. Just *marvellous*!" Scarlet-faced Mr Donkin threw his baton onto the floor in exasperation. "Well done for disbanding the Compton Poppleford Choir in one fell swoop, Mrs Churchill!"

"I did nothing of the sort," she replied as the last few members left the room. "I merely asked you to stop speaking to them in that rude manner."

"I've always spoken to them like that, and no one ever questioned it until you turned up!"

"You're a revolutionary, Mrs Churchill," said Pemberley proudly.

"Now you put it like that, I suppose I am, aren't I?" Churchill smoothed down her twinset with both hands.

Everyone except Mr Donkin and the two ladies had exited the room. The choirmaster pulled angrily at his festive cravat, as if to cool himself down.

"You're making me extremely hot under the collar, Mrs Churchill!"

"Hot under the cravat, you mean."

"Yes, that as well!" He adjusted it slightly, then bent down to pick up his baton. "Eh? Where's it gone?"

Churchill looked beyond him and caught sight of Oswald sprawled in an easy chair beside the fireplace with the baton in his mouth.

"I think Miss Pemberley's dog has found it, Mr Donkin."

"What? Where?!" He spun around in a circle. "I don't see a dog."

"He's in that chair beside the fire."

There was a loud splintering crack as Oswald's teeth chomped through the baton.

Mr Donkin let out a cry as he dashed across the oriental rug toward the chair. The little dog leapt away before the choirmaster reached him and scampered out of the door.

"The little blighter!" fumed Mr Donkin as he picked up the two pieces of chewed baton. "Forty years old, that was! And made from the finest maple wood!"

"Well, you have two of them now," observed Pemberley.

"Are you trying to be funny with me, woman?"

"Now, now. There's no need to speak to my aide-de-camp in that tone of voice, Mr Donkin," said Churchill.

"Why ever not? Thanks to you two and your flea-ridden mutt I now have neither a choir nor a baton!"

"I do apologise for the rather sudden change in your circumstances, Mr Donkin. It certainly wasn't our intention to produce this outcome when we first arrived on the scene. Perhaps if you hadn't thrown your baton onto the floor in a fit of temper the dog wouldn't have laid ahold of it."

The choirmaster strode over to them and pointed a splintered half-baton at Churchill. "I'll make sure you pay for this, Mrs Churchill, oh yes I will! You'll regret the day you ever set foot in here for the Vicarage Christmas Party!"

"I'm quite sure I was already regretting it before I encountered you, Mr Donkin. I've never known such sparse catering at a party." She glanced around the parlour with great disappointment. "Do you mind me asking where you got your mince pie from earlier?"

"Yes!" he retorted.

"I see. We'll be on our way then, won't we, Miss Pemberley? We'll find that mince pie mountain yet."

Chapter Five

Mr Hurricks's booming voice drifted down the corridor as the two ladies resumed their search for food.

"Good grief, Pembers, is that man still droning on?"

"Yes, and I think he's only up to the Ghost of Christmas Past. There are two more ghosts to go."

Churchill and Pemberley reached the music room and saw that it was almost full, with the choir's former members having taken up residence there. The vicar was chatting to Mrs Thonnings beside the harp.

"If anyone's going to know where the food is it's the vicar, isn't it?" Churchill said to her assistant.

"Mrs Churchill! Miss Pemberley!" chimed the vicar as they approached. "I'm so glad to see you've put your dog in the yard, where he can cause no further trouble."

"Have we?" replied Churchill.

"Isn't that where he is?"

"Oh."

Churchill and Pemberley exchanged a look, which confirmed that neither had any idea where Oswald had got to.

"Erm, yes. That's where he'll be, Vicar," Churchill said hopefully.

"Jolly good."

"Why aren't you listening to Mr Hurricks, Mrs Churchill?" Mrs Thonnings asked.

"We could ask the same thing of you," replied Churchill.

"Oh, I've heard him before. I forget how many vicarage Christmas parties I've attended to date, but there have been many. This is your first one, isn't it?"

"It is indeed, but I was just wondering—"

"Then why aren't you listening to Mr Hurricks? It's a festive rite of passage for all new Compton Poppleforders."

The vicar gave a laugh. "It is indeed! The rest of us have heard him countless times, of course. Including you, I believe, Miss Pemberley?"

"Oh yes. I have very much served my time in the recital arena."

Churchill felt a pang of envy.

"I think he's only just finished the first ghost," said the vicar. "If you hop back in there now, Mrs Churchill, you won't have missed out on too much. And hopefully Mr Hurricks won't even notice."

"He keeps score of these things, does he?"

"Oh yes!"

"I see. Well, I have no objection to listening to *A Christmas Carol*, but the experience would be all the more palatable if I could furnish myself with a little plate of something. An egg and cucumber sandwich, perhaps. And then maybe a slice of cheese and a small bunch of grapes followed by a mince pie or two. In fact, I've heard all about the legendary mince pie mountain. I'd be more than happy to skip the sandwich, cheese and grapes and go straight for a mince pie."

The vicar laughed again. "That's probably just as well. I don't think Mrs Robertson prepared any egg and cucumber sandwiches."

"Where is the mince pie mountain, out of interest?"

"It's being replenished as we speak," replied the vicar.

"In the meantime, you'd better go and listen to Mr Hurricks," urged Mrs Thonnings.

Churchill felt a snap of irritation. "Are you trying to get rid of me, Mrs Thonnings?"

She took a step back in surprise. "Goodness me, no! I would never do such a thing. I simply wouldn't want you to miss out on the rite of—"

"It's quite all right. I shall go and listen to Mr Hurricks forthwith."

The vicar checked his watch. "Gosh! The orphans will be here shortly."

"Orphans?"

"Yes. I've invited the children and staff from the local orphanage to join us here, and we've prepared some lovely surprises for them. They've had such a difficult year and are in dire need of cheering up. The orphanage has no spare funds to celebrate Christmas properly, so Mrs Thonnings has arranged for each child to receive a Christmas gift, and I shall ask Mr Donkin if his choir can put on a special performance for them. I think two or three Christmas songs would cheer them up immensely."

"Oh dear," said Pemberley.

"Why do you say that?" asked the vicar.

Pemberley turned to face Churchill. "Er…"

"You may need to speak to Mr Donkin sooner rather than later, Vicar," said Churchill.

"Oh, I see. Is there some sort of problem?"

"None at all, other than I think I overheard him say

that he would probably be leaving shortly, so you might want to let him know what you require of the choir."

"Require of the choir. That rhymes!" giggled Mrs Thonnings.

"So it does," said Churchill.

"Talking of rhyming, you've written some poetry, haven't you, Mrs Churchill?" said Pemberley.

"That may be so, but let's not bore the vicar with talk of it now, Miss Pemberley. He needs to speak to Mr Donkin, doesn't he?"

"Oh yes, so he does. There may no longer be a choir, after all!"

"I beg your pardon," said the vicar. "Did you say there may no longer be a choir?"

"No, no," interjected Churchill. "Come along now, Miss Pemberley. Let's allow the vicar and Mr Donkin to discuss it between themselves. It's high time we went and listened to Mr Hurricks. He must be on the second ghost by now."

The vicar gave a polite nod and strolled away.

"I don't really feel the need to go to the recital," said Pemberley.

Churchill gritted her teeth. "Aren't you the lucky one, Pembers?"

"I think I'll go and find Oswald," she replied, "out in the yard."

"Oh yes, you go and see him *out in the yard*. And once you've done that, perhaps you could seek out the replenished mince pie mountain and bring me in a pie or five."

"Would Mr Hurricks mind his performance being interrupted, do you think?"

"I couldn't care less what Mr Hurricks thinks, quite frankly. Unless he's happy for one of his audience members to faint from lack of sustenance I think he should allow everyone to bring in a generous plate of mince pies or whatever other foodstuffs they require."

～

There were noticeably fewer people in the drawing room than there had been earlier, so Churchill managed to squeeze herself onto the end of a plush-looking sofa next to a man in a tartan jacket. She soon realised that he liked to applaud the story at regular intervals, and each time he did so his right elbow jabbed into her side. She placed her handbag firmly on her lap and resigned herself to her uncomfortable fate.

Mr Hurricks was still in full flow, his theatrical voice rising and falling with the story. He adopted various postures for the different characters, with Ebenezer Scrooge's dialogue delivered from a stooped position with an embittered, twisted face. The person most enjoying this rendition of *A Christmas Carol* appeared to be Mr Hurricks himself.

The room's occupants seemed to be carefully monitoring the moments when Mr Hurricks was most distracted by his craft and would take those opportunities to dart out through the drawing room door unnoticed. On two occasions they weren't quite quick enough and were summoned back and admonished by Mr Hurricks for attempting to leave halfway through his performance.

The tartan-jacketed man continued with his elbow-jabbing applause, and Churchill felt a great sense of accomplishment when Mr Hurricks reached the third ghost in the story: the Ghost of Christmas Yet to Come. Her thoughts returned to the mince pies yet to come.

What was keeping Pemberley? Had Oswald got himself into trouble again?

A haughty-faced Mr Hurricks was busy pointing his finger at the audience as he played the part of the Ghost of Christmas Yet to Come when a loud scream resounded throughout the vicarage.

Members of the audience jumped in surprise and glanced around, wide-eyed. Some began to mutter.

"Quiet!" hissed Mr Hurricks. "There's a performance in progress!"

The scream rang out again, and Churchill realised quickly that it was more than high Christmas spirits. She rose up from the sofa.

"Sit down!" Mr Hurricks commanded those who had left their seats.

"But someone's screaming," said an old lady wearing a Christmas hat.

"She's probably just had a little too much sherry," replied Mr Hurricks. "Do not disturb the performance!"

Churchill tentatively placed her behind back on the sofa and glanced anxiously at the door. Her immediate concern was that Oswald had done something unforgivable. *Had he bitten someone again?* The thought worried her terribly, but she reassured herself with the fact that Pemberley would have to deal with it.

Mr Hurricks was just raising his ghostly finger again when an even clearer sound rang out.

"Murder!" cried the voice. "There's been a murder!"

Nothing Mr Hurricks did could keep the audience in their seats after that. There were shouts and shrieks, and a general melee ensued. Churchill bounced out of her seat this time and scrambled her way through the door.

Chapter Six

OUT IN THE CORRIDOR, a hysterical Mrs Stonecastle was in floods of tears. Pemberley stood close by, a stunned expression on her face and a plate of mince pies in her hand.

"Murder, you say?" asked Churchill. "Did you cry '*Murder!*', Mrs Stonecastle?"

"Yes!"

"But whom? And where?"

"Down there!" she wailed, pointing down the corridor. "In the parlour!"

"Come along, Pembers," said Churchill. "We haven't a moment to lose!"

"I'll be along in a moment, Mrs Churchill. Mrs Stonecastle is rather distressed and I think she needs someone to remain with her."

"Very well. That's a good idea."

Churchill turned on her heel and charged down the corridor before pausing outside the door to the parlour.

What terrible scene would greet her from within?

She took a deep breath, then entered.

At first glance the room appeared to be empty, a fire

burning cheerfully in the grate. However, lying face-down in the middle of the oriental rug was a man wearing dark trousers and a festive waistcoat. Churchill carefully edged forward, her heart pounding. It was then that she saw something shiny sticking out of his back.

The ornamental hilt of a knife.

Churchill gave a loud gasp.

The man's head lay to one side, his eyes wide open and staring at the fire.

"It can't be true," she muttered to herself. "It's Mr Donkin!"

She bent down hesitantly to feel for a pulse at his wrist, but there was none.

Churchill rose to her feet and turned to see that a small group of people had gathered in the doorway.

The vicar stepped forward, his face ashen. "Can he be saved?" he asked.

"I don't think so, Vicar. Someone appears to have murdered him. We'll need a doctor to look him over, though. Dr Bratchett is the village doctor, isn't he?"

"Yes, that's right."

"Here I am," announced a small, rotund man as he pushed his way into the room. "What do we have here, then? Oh dear! He doesn't look very well, does he?"

"He's been murdered, Doctor," said the vicar.

"It certainly appears that way. He couldn't have inflicted that injury on himself, could he?"

"And I do believe the weapon belongs to me," added the vicar. "Someone's gone and stabbed him with my ornamental letter opener!"

"Dear oh dear," said the doctor as he knelt down beside the deceased choirmaster. He moved him gently as he began to examine the body. "He's dead all right."

"But when did it happen?" asked the vicar. "And how?"

"I'd say that it happened quite recently," said Dr Bratchett, "perhaps within the past half-hour. Do you know when he was last seen alive?"

"I shall make some enquiries," announced Churchill.

"We'd best leave it to the police," replied the doctor. "Has anyone called the inspector yet?"

"I'll make sure he's summoned," said the vicar.

"It'll take Mappin a while to get out here in this snowfall," commented the doctor.

"I'll have everything in hand until then," said Churchill.

The doctor looked up at her from his kneeling position beside the corpse. "You're that private detective lady, aren't you?"

"Yes, that's right," she replied proudly.

"I've heard about you."

"All good, I hope?"

The doctor gave no reply as he set about examining the choirmaster's body again.

"Well, I shall do what I can until the police inspector arrives," said Churchill. "In the meantime, the scene needs to be preserved."

"Ah yes, you're quite right there," replied the doctor, standing to his feet. "Everybody out of the room, please. The killer may have left an important clue, and it'll be impossible to find it if everyone goes trampling all over the place."

There were tearful expressions and mutterings of shock as people left the room. Churchill pushed past them, looking for Pemberley and Mrs Stonecastle. She found them seated close to the harpsichord in the music room. The plate of mince pies sat untouched on Pemberley's lap.

"Terrible news, isn't it?" Churchill said. "I can't say

that I warmed to the man, but there was no need for someone to go and murder him."

"Awful!" replied Mrs Stonecastle, wringing her hands.

"Mrs Stonecastle has just been telling me how she came to discover his body," said Pemberley.

"I felt a bit sorry for him after we all walked out," she explained, her eyes wet and rimmed with red. "So I mulled things over while eating a mince pie, and then decided to go and find him again to see if he was all right. It was then that I stumbled upon that terrible scene."

"And that's when you started screaming," added Pemberley.

"Yes, that's right, I couldn't help myself, you see! I've never seen a murdered person before. To begin with I wondered whether it was some sort of odd joke, but when I saw that he wasn't moving I realised the knife in his back had to be real."

"Did you notice anyone leaving the parlour as you made your way there?" asked Churchill.

"No. In fact, I doubted whether Mr Donkin would still be in the parlour as I headed back there. I remember wondering whether he'd gone home in a sulk. I still can't believe he's dead! It was only a short while ago that he was shouting at us all."

"It was indeed."

"One moment he was shouting at us, the next he was dead!"

Mrs Stonecastle crumpled into a fresh flow of tears. While Pemberley comforted her, Churchill eyed the plate of mince pies on her lap, reluctantly deciding that it was not an appropriate time to tuck into one.

A bell tinkled. "Will everyone come into the drawing room, please?" announced the vicar. "I need to speak to you all."

Mrs Thonnings latched herself on to Churchill as they made their way toward the drawing room.

"Who did it, Mrs Churchill?" Her eyes were wide with wonder. "Who could have plunged a knife into the choirmaster's back?"

"Your guess is as good as mine, Mrs Thonnings."

"But you're the detective. What are your initial thoughts?"

"I'll need to make some enquiries first. I'm as clueless as you are at present."

"Surely not?"

"I'm afraid so."

Everyone filed into the drawing room in stunned silence. Mr Hurricks sat slumped in a chair with his arms folded, angered that his performance had been so rudely interrupted.

The vicar stood in front of the Christmas tree and addressed them all. "For the first time ever in the Vicarage Christmas Party's eighty-four-year history, I am saddened to inform you that a guest has been cruelly murdered in the most despicable manner. I'm sure most of you are aware by now that the deceased gentleman is, I mean *was*, the choirmaster of Compton Poppleford Choir, and I'm sure you will join me in passing your condolences on to all members of the choir. Mr Bob Donkin was one of the proverbial pillars of our esteemed community, and when one such pillar topples the entire pediment is in danger of falling down. However, we can join together to support the pediment during these troubled times. We must not let it fall on our heads! Now, let's spend a moment praying for our dearly departed friend."

Everyone bowed their heads and listened as the vicar prayed. After the final amen had been uttered, a man with a large nose called out, "Where's the killer?"

"He'll be long gone by now," replied the vicar.

"He might not be. He might be hiding in our midst!" the man replied.

Mutters of concern spread among the guests.

"What if he murders someone else?" a lady with scarlet lipstick and buck teeth cried.

"I should think that very unlikely," replied the vicar, "and even if he did, he'd have to find another murder weapon because the original one remains embedded in Mr Donkin's back."

Several gasps of shock could be heard around the room.

"What about a piece of lead piping?" a man with mutton-chop whiskers called out. "He could use that!"

"Or how about a candlestick?" suggested the lady with buck teeth.

"Do you have any loose pipes, Vicar?" asked the whiskered man.

"No I don't, and stop giving the chap ideas," replied the vicar. "If the killer is still hiding in our midst, he'll hear your suggestions for alternative murder weapons! The next thing we know he'll be looking for lead pipes or candlesticks lying around so he can continue his murder quest."

"I hardly think we're talking about a rampant, half-crazed murderer here, Vicar," Churchill interjected.

"I beg to differ, Mrs Churchill. The man has already carried out one senseless act. He must be completely crazed!"

"What I meant to say, Vicar," she replied, stepping forward, "is that the murderer must have had a motive for murdering Mr Donkin. That motive will either have been money, passion or revenge."

"There are more motives than that," the old lady in the Christmas hat argued.

"Such as?" asked Churchill.

"Inheritance!"

"That comes under money."

"Revenge!" another voice called out.

"Exactly, we've already said that one. The question is, who was set to benefit from Mr Donkin's death?"

"No one," said a lady in a frilly blue dress.

"Was he wealthy?" asked Churchill.

The crowd conferred among themselves but no one appeared to know.

"Did he have any offspring?"

"No, there was no fruit from his loins!" the man with the mutton-chop whiskers called out.

The thought of the choirmaster's loins turned Churchill's stomach a little. "Does anyone know whom he might have named in his will?" she asked. "Or if he even left a will, for that matter?"

"Mrs Brunton might know," said the vicar.

"Who's she?"

"His housekeeper."

"Revenge!" came the shout again.

"I heard you the first time," said Churchill. "Who keeps saying that?"

"Why should anyone want to murder Mr Donkin out of revenge?" asked the vicar. "He was a thoroughly decent chap."

"If you say so, Vicar," replied Churchill.

The tartan-jacketed man stepped forward. "There's rather a lot of talk going on here and not a great deal being done. I realise we're waiting for the police to arrive, but in the meantime we could send out a search party to look for the murderer. There's thick snow out there, so we could just follow his footprints!"

"A marvellous idea, Mr Fordbridge!" said the vicar.

"How will we know whether they're the right foot-prints?" asked Churchill.

"There can't be many out there," replied Mr Ford-bridge. "Most of us have been inside the vicarage all evening, and the snow's been falling thick and fast all the while. All we need do is look for a set of footprints leading away from the vicarage. An unaccompanied set of foot-prints, as the murderer is likely to have fled alone. And quite widely spaced, as he would have been running. He'd have wanted to make a quick getaway, wouldn't he? We could start by looking below the parlour window ledge. That's probably the most likely escape route, isn't it? He probably jumped out of the window and ran down the hill, leaving a clear set of prints for us to follow!"

"What great thinking, Mr Fordbridge," said the vicar. "You should consider becoming a detective!"

The tartan-jacketed gentleman gave a proud smile.

"It *is* quite good thinking," added Churchill, "but being a detective takes a little more than *quite good thinking*."

"It's the best suggestion I've heard so far," said the vicar. "Now, let's go and find those footprints!"

Everyone got up to leave just as a dozen or so wan-looking children in hats and scarves appeared at the door. They were accompanied by a prim-looking lady in a navy hat and a matching fitted jacket.

"Oh, it's the orphans," said the vicar. "I'd forgotten about them."

"Is everything all right?" asked the prim lady.

"I'm afraid not, Miss Pauling," replied the vicar. "Something rather singular and untoward has occurred."

"Oh dear," she replied. "Is the party cancelled?"

"Not for the children," replied the vicar. "They were expecting Christmas gifts, so we must honour that. Please take them into the music room, where Mrs Thonnings will entertain them for now. We must pretend that everything is as normal."

"Goodness!" replied Miss Pauling. "That sounds most unfortunate, whatever it is. We shall go into the music room as instructed. The children are already quite tired, as we've just been playing outside in the snow. They wanted to make snowmen and have a snowball fight before we came inside."

The vicar's face fell. "You mean to say they've been trampling all over the snow out there?"

"Yes, they were terribly excited to see so much of it. Is there a problem?"

"No, no problem at all. I'll come and see you all in the music room shortly, Miss Pauling," he said as she departed.

"Mr Fordbridge," said the vicar. "Can you round up a few men to have a look for the murderer's footprints? Men only, of course. We wouldn't want any ladies becoming involved in a confrontation with a cold-blooded killer."

"Yo ho ho! I has the puddin'!" sang out a jolly voice. "Line up! Line up! It's time to pass the puddin'! Yo ho ho!"

Father Christmas stood in the doorway with a layer of melting snowflakes on his shoulders and hat.

"Oh, hello there, Donald," said the vicar. "I'm afraid—"

"Donald? Who's Donald? I'm Father Christmas, and I has the puddin'! Line up! Line up! It's time to pass the puddin'!"

The vicar grimaced and walked over to him. "Donald, may I have a quiet word?"

The two men stepped out of the room together.

"I'm not holding out much hope of anyone finding the murderer's footprints now that a dozen children have used the vicarage garden as a snow-filled playground," muttered

Churchill to Pemberley. "Everything will be quite churned over."

"If there were any in the first place," added Pemberley. "I didn't notice any when I was out there with Oswald."

"What were you doing out there with Oswald?"

"I went to find him while you were listening to Mr Hurricks's performance. And there he was, playing in the snow. He's never seen snow before."

"He wasn't in the yard, then?"

"No."

"And where is he now?"

"Drying off upstairs somewhere. It wouldn't surprise me if he's found himself a nice comfortable bed to lie on. That's what he does at home."

"He'd better be careful the vicar doesn't find him up there. Can you imagine how upset the vicar would be if he found a wet dog on his bed? It would probably finish him off."

Chapter Seven

WHILE THE VICAR was out speaking to Father Christmas an idea formed in Churchill's mind. "I detect an opportunity to investigate the scene in a little more detail, Pembers. It's the last chance we'll have before Mappin gets here. You know what he's like; he'll refuse to share any of the details with us, then accuse us of meddling and so on and so forth."

The two ladies sidled out of the drawing room and made their way down the corridor toward the parlour. The parlour door had been closed, so Churchill checked that no one had spotted them before carefully opening it again. As she stepped inside, she saw that Mr Donkin's body had been covered with an overcoat. Despite this, Churchill still felt a shiver up her spine as they surveyed the scene, with the fire burning low in the grate.

"Now then, Pembers, tread carefully. We're looking for clues."

The two ladies looked down at the polished floorboards and rug, hoping to find something the murderer might have dropped.

"How annoying that there are no obvious ones lying around," said Churchill. "You'd think there might be a watch or a locket or an earring or something that could instantly give away the murderer's identity."

"There's nothing here," said Pemberley. "Nothing to go on at all. That's another nice selection of books over there, though." She started walking toward a bookcase on the far side of the fireplace. "There are several here that I'd like to borrow."

"Enough, Pembers!" hissed Churchill. "We've got to look carefully at the crime scene to see what clues we can find. Look, here's the window the murderer must have used to escape."

She stepped closer to the window, across which a large pair of velvet curtains had been drawn.

"Now I'm sure these curtains were closed when we were in here earlier," she stated.

"Yes, I think they were," replied Pemberley as she joined her.

Churchill pushed them aside. "Well then, if the murderer left hurriedly through the window, he somehow found the time to draw the curtains and close the window again."

"And lock the window from the inside."

"Really, Pembers?"

"Yes, look. The latch has been pulled across, but you can only do that from the inside."

"Goodness! So you can. That means either someone came in here after the murderer had escaped through the window, pushed the latch to and closed the curtains, or…"

"Or the murderer didn't leave through the window."

"In which case the only exit would have been through the door we've just entered by."

"Or via the chimney."

"Only the fire has been lit all evening," said Churchill. "I clearly recall it from when we encountered Mr Donkin in here with the choir. And besides, even if there hadn't been a fire it would have been impossible for the murderer to escape up the chimney unless he were a small child or a monkey."

"It's not unheard of. Atkins had a case like that once."

"I can imagine he did." Churchill pulled the curtains back across the window. "The murderer could be a member of the choir," she suggested.

"Oh gosh, yes. He could, couldn't he? Perhaps he murdered Mr Donkin after the choirmaster shouted at them."

"A slight overreaction to being shouted at, one might argue. Then again, we are talking about a murderer here. They're not exactly known for their restraint and moral character, are they?"

"And stabbed in the back, too," added Pemberley. "What a cowardly act."

"That's a good point, Pembers. It suggests Mr Donkin was facing away from his assailant when the blow was struck. He might not even have seen him."

"Or perhaps they initially engaged in conversation, but when it reached its conclusion Mr Donkin turned away and it was then that the killer struck."

"With the vicar's ornamental letter opener. The killer didn't bring his own weapon to the party."

"Suggesting it was an impulsive act," said Pemberley.

"It does, doesn't it? Gosh, I think we're getting quite good at this murder-solving business, aren't we? We've been able to come up with a range of ideas based on the limited information available to us. The culprit may not have come to the party intending to murder the choirmaster, but something happened here to provoke him, so he availed himself of the vicar's letter opener."

"But where did he pick it up from?"

"Where indeed? We shall have to ask the vicar where he left it. I remember him using it to open the envelope containing the name of the Christmas cake competition prize-winner. But where did he leave it after that?"

Churchill closed her eyes as she tried to recall the scene.

"He announced Mrs Stonecastle as the winner, didn't he?" she said. "And then you and I grumbled about the fact that there was no cake for us to eat. And after that Mr Hurricks began his recital. So where did the vicar go then? And where did he put his letter opener?"

"He may not have put it anywhere."

"But he must have done in order for the murderer to have laid hold of it."

"Perhaps he *is* the murderer."

"Oh, Pembers!" Churchill clapped her hands together. "He could well be. What a thought! But don't you recall him saying that he couldn't understand why anyone would want to murder Mr Donkin because he was such a decent chap?"

"It could have been a bluff," replied Pemberley. "Perhaps he really despised the man."

"Well yes, I suppose it could have been a bluff. He may have been lying purely to mislead us. Goodness, Pembers, what a shocking thought! Just a moment, though. The vicar wouldn't use his own letter opener to commit the murder, would he? That would be foolish, because everyone would immediately assume that he was the culprit."

"Quite the opposite, in fact."

"Really? How so?"

"Yes! No one even suspects the vicar yet, despite his letter opener being used as the murder weapon."

"Ah, yes! Good point."

"So the vicar may be relying on his profession as a man of the cloth as a means of protecting himself. This theory can be summarised thus: firstly, no one would believe that a vicar would stab the choirmaster with his letter opener because he's a vicar. Secondly, no one would believe that a murderer would kill someone using a weapon that so obviously belongs to himself."

"I think you're beginning to lose me a little there, Pembers, but I get the general gist of what you're saying. Put simply, the vicar is the obvious culprit. Almost too obvious, some might say."

"But protected by the fact that he's a vicar, so no one suspects him."

"Too obvious and no one suspects him. Right, I'm really lost now. Is he a suspect or not?"

"He must be considered one."

"Yes indeed. As must everyone, I suppose. Oh dear, Pembers. For a moment there I thought we were making progress, but I find myself befuddled by all this reasoning. What's happened to your plate of mince pies, by the way?"

"I left them with Mrs Stonecastle."

"Oh dear. I suppose she may have eaten them in that case."

"If so, she deserved every one of them. She was in terrible shock after discovering Mr Donkin lying dead here."

"Or she may have lost her appetite altogether," suggested Churchill hopefully. "Shock can cause people to go one of two ways. Where did you get them from, anyway?"

"From the mince pie mountain in the morning room."

"Bravo! Lead me to it, Pembers! Lead me to it right away! I think a mince pie break is much needed, and after that we can return here and continue with our sleuthing. With any luck we'll have this case solved before the local constabulary turns up!"

Churchill felt her heart plummet as they stepped out of the parlour and saw the familiar brown-whiskered and blue-uniformed figure of Inspector Mappin striding toward them with the vicar by his side and a number of stragglers in tow.

"I might have known it!" declared the inspector as soon as he set eyes on Churchill and Pemberley. "What have you been doing in there?"

"Just examining the scene, Inspector. And a good evening to you, too," replied Churchill.

"Meddling with the scene, more like. Did you touch anything?"

"Nothing at all."

"Good. You weren't supposed to be in there! Why did you let the two of them loose, Vicar?"

"I didn't realise they intended to go in there. We were outside looking for the murderer's footprints in the snow, you see, and I trusted that everyone would stay away from the murder scene until you arrived."

"I'm afraid you underestimated the snooping beak of Mrs Churchill."

"Snooping? *Beak?*" protested Churchill. "I'm a private detective, Inspector, and I decided to get cracking on the case while we waited for the tardy local constabulary to turn up."

"And what progress have you made with the case so far, Mrs Churchill?"

"We've come up with several theories, haven't we, Miss Pemberley?"

"We certainly have."

Inspector Mappin gave a loud huff through his nose.

Churchill knew there was no need to remind him of the fact that her theories had solved cases in the past.

"Anyway, we're just off for a well-earned break, Inspector. Good luck with the case."

"What are the theories you've come up with?"

"Oh, just a few here and there. We're not at liberty to share them until we've worked them up into fully coherent…"

"Suppositions," added Pemberley.

"Yes, those."

"And postulations."

"Lots of those, too."

"Hot air, more like," retorted Mappin.

"And hot air, too. Lots of that. Best of luck tracking down the culprit, Inspector!"

Chapter Eight

"Let's leave that hapless police officer to get on with it while we sit down with a little plate of something, Pembers. I can't even begin to explain how hungry I am now; I honestly don't know how my body has managed to sustain itself. I'm actually quite surprised that I'm still alive! I'm delighted you found the mince pie mountain in the morning room earlier. Now, where is the morning room?"

"It's just along this way."

Churchill mustered up all the strength she had left to follow Pemberley. On the way there they passed the children in the music room and glanced in to see Mrs Thonnings performing an interesting rendition of '*The Jolly Tinker*'.

"Goodness!" whispered Churchill as they went on their way. "That's a rather bawdy song for young minds, isn't it?"

"That's Mrs Thonnings for you. She only knows bawdy songs."

"You'd think that a lady who owns a haberdashery

shop would have wanted to perform something a little more erudite."

"I blame the sherry, and I'm afraid it's only going to get worse. We'll have to go in there and remove her before she gets to '*Keyhole in the Door*'."

"Do we have enough time to feast on a mince pie or five before then?"

"Just about."

When they reached the morning room, Churchill was most perturbed to find the door closed and a constable standing in front of it.

"Excuse me, Constable. We just need to step inside to fetch a little plate of something."

"No can do, I'm afraid."

"That's entirely the wrong response, Constable. I'd like to hear something more along the lines of, 'Do please step inside, ladies, and avail yourself of the refreshments within.'"

"The answer's no."

"*No?* Why *no?* This is the morning room, is it not? It's where all the food is, including the mince pie mountain! Have you any idea how long I've been waiting to clap eyes on the mince pie mountain? Any idea at all?"

He shook his head. "No."

"All evening, that's how long."

"And a bit of late afternoon as well," added Pemberley.

"Exactly! Now, will you please let us in, Constable?"

"'Fraid not."

"Why not?"

"Because it's closed to the public."

"Why? Who on earth closed it?"

"Inspector Mappin."

Churchill gave a bitter groan. "I should have known! If only we'd come to the morning room before starting work on the murder case. You do realise, Constable, that we've been doing your superior's work for him, don't you? We didn't have to, you know. Oh no! We could have happily filled our faces in the morning room instead, like everyone else at this accursed party!"

"Why has Inspector Mappin closed the morning room, Constable?" asked Pemberley.

"To preserve the scene."

"What scene?" queried Churchill. "A scene of plates sitting there piled high with sandwiches, hams, cheeses, mince pies and… Oh, goodness, I can hardly bear it!"

Pemberley moved to Churchill's side and supported her arm.

"There, there, Mrs Churchill. We'll find you something to eat yet."

"Not if the vicar or that wretched Mappin have anything to do with it. Are they trying to starve me sense-less? I fear they are, Pembers. They're trying to starve an old lady out of Compton Poppleford in the vain hope that she'll return to Richmond-upon-Thames. But I tell you what, Pembers. I won't stand for it! I won't stand for it a moment longer!"

"Mrs Churchill, I think you need a little sit-down."

"I need food, Pembers, food! Is there any chance, Constable, that you could quickly pop beyond the closed door and fill a plate for me? Just mince pies will do if you need to be quick, although a nice slice of cheese would be quite pleasant if there's time for it. I'm rather partial to a piece of Red Windsor. Have you ever tried it?"

"No."

"No you haven't tried it, or no you're not willing to fetch me a little plate of something?"

"Both."

Churchill dropped her handbag onto the floor and

slumped back against the wall. "Oh Pemberley, I could weep."

"We'll go down to the kitchens, Mrs Churchill. I'm sure the cook and her staff will find you something to eat."

Pemberley picked up Churchill's handbag and handed it to her.

"I hope so; I'm almost done for. At this rate there will be two deaths at the Vicarage Christmas Party this year. That's not a particularly festive thought, is it?"

"Before we go, Constable," ventured Pemberley, "perhaps you could tell us why Inspector Mappin is preserving the scene in the morning room. Has something been found in there?"

"Yes, an important piece of evidence, I believe."

"What does he know?" scoffed Churchill. "He's only just arrived. How can he tell whether there's important evidence in the morning room or not?"

The constable gave a shrug.

~

"I do believe you're the kindest woman I have ever met, Mrs Robertson," stated Churchill as she seated herself at the large oak table in the basement kitchen and tucked into a freshly baked loaf.

"Oh, fie! It's only a bit o' bread," replied the cook as she wiped her hands on her apron.

"It may only be a bit of bread to you, but to me it's the finest manna from the great heavens above."

"Lordy, is that right, missus?"

"I'm afraid Mrs Churchill becomes rather verbose when she's hungry," said Pemberley. "She should return to normal once the nourishing effects of the bread have made themselves known."

"I'm only sorry I ain't got no mince pies down 'ere," said the cook. "Fancy that inspector lockin' 'em in a room! Now no one can get to 'em and all me mince pies is goin' to waste."

"They could at least have removed the food before sealing the room, couldn't they?" said Pemberley. "Unless the important piece of evidence the constable referred to happens to be something consumable."

"How can a bit o' food be 'portan' evidence?" asked the cook.

"I've no idea," replied Pemberley.

"Only Inspector Mappin knows," said Churchill, "and he's the most lunk-headed, goose-brained clodpole I've ever had the misfortune to come across."

"You can't say them things 'bout the inspector!" remonstrated the cook.

"Oh yes I can. He locked away all the food! He's a half-witted, jolt-headed—"

"Why don't you concentrate on eating your bread for the time being, Mrs Churchill?" suggested Pemberley. "That way you'll soon begin to feel a little better."

"And now we got this terrible murder on our 'ands," said the cook. "At Christmas time an' all!"

"Did you know Mr Donkin well?" asked Pemberley.

"Only a bit," replied the cook. "'E's lived in the village all 'is life, ain't 'e? 'Part from the war, o' course. He wen' away for that, like most of 'em did. Never married. Not after all that business wiv the Prussian princess."

"I remember it well," replied Pemberley.

"Excuse me!" exclaimed Churchill, a little surprised. "Mr Donkin and a Prussian princess?"

"Oh, it ain't nothin' but an old fairy tale now," said the cook. "Quite a sad one, though, ain't it, Miss Pemberley?"

Miss Pemberley gave a hearty nod.

"Do tell," said Churchill, carving another slice off the loaf. "How on earth did the village choirmaster meet a Prussian princess?"

"He weren't the choirmaster at the time. 'E worked down the post office wiv 'is father. Donkin Senior were the postmaster."

"And the Prussian princess popped into the post office, did she?"

"No, he's met 'er over in Paris."

"What was he doing there?"

"He wen' over there with 'is brother to see the sights for a few days an' 'e bumped into 'er on the top o' the Eiffel Tower. Love at first sight, it were."

"Is that so?"

"The story goes as they was insep'rable for the followin' days strollin' round them little streets they got there."

"That's actually rather a romantic tale." Churchill remembered Mr Donkin admonishing his choir and struggled to imagine the same man walking the streets of Paris with his lady love. "But then it all went wrong, did it?"

"Yeah, 'fraid so. When the time come to part she's confessed to Bob as her father'd betrothed her to annuva man. A princelin' o' some sort."

"Oh dear. And that was the end of that, I suppose. He never fell in love again, then?"

"No. She were 'is one and only true love."

"Well, I suppose it couldn't be helped. When one is the daughter of a Prussian aristocrat one doesn't have a great deal of influence when it comes to one's marriage partner."

"Poor Mr Donkin," said Pemberley. "And then his twin brother was killed in the war."

"Yeah, 'e were an' all. 'Ector Donkin," said the cook. "'E were a scoundrel, though, weren't 'e? I shouldn't speak ill o' the dead, but there weren't no one as missed 'im after 'e died."

"What sort of scoundrelly things did he do?" asked Churchill.

"'E stole money from 'is father's post office an' seduced the cabinet maker's daughter, then 'e's went back on 'is promise to marry her."

"What a rotten scoundrel!"

"'E were a shockin' scoundrel!"

"Didn't the Prussian princess come to Compton Poppleford in a bid to track Mr Donkin down?" said Pemberley.

"Yeah, she did an' all! I'd forgotten that bit o' the story. 'Bout a month after they'd parted ways in Paris she's arrived at the Donkin 'ome in this very village, claiming as she'd escaped the clutches of 'er father and the princelin'."

"Really?"

"Yeah, and she were after elopin' wiv Bob Donkin!"

"Goodness!"

"But only 'Ector Donkin were at 'ome 'cause the others was busy workin' down the post office, see. He told 'er to wait by the pack'orse bridge just 'alf a mile out the village and said 'e'd tell Bob to meet 'er there, soon as 'e'd finished 'is work. Said 'e thought it best if she stayed out the village, away from the gossipin' villagers. A Prussian princess in a little Dorset village 'as a way o' turnin' a few 'eads, you know."

"I should imagine so. Was she a beauty?"

"Oh yeah, quite a beauty she were. They always are, though, ain't they?"

"Yes, I suppose so."

"Anyways, the long and short of it's that Bob Donkin come 'ome from 'is shift and 'is brother ain't never breathed a single word of the princess who was there waitin' for 'im down the pack'orse bridge."

"Surely not!"

"'Fraid so."

"What a good-for-nothing charlatan! Why didn't he tell his brother she had turned up out of the blue?"

"'E were proberly jealous an' couldn't bear to see 'is brother 'appy. 'E might even 'ave 'ad designs on the princess 'imself."

Churchill gasped. "Dreadful man! Did poor Bob Donkin ever see the princess again?"

"No, 'e never."

"I wonder what became of her. The poor lady was forced to wait there beside the packhorse bridge for a lover who never arrived. She must have been terribly upset. Did Bob ever find out that she had come looking for him?"

"She did, yeah. The old manservant's wen' and told 'im the followin' day."

"The old manservant was there when she called at the house, was he?"

"Yeah. 'E used to pretend 'e were deaf so as people'd talk freely around 'im, assuming 'e couldn't 'ear nothin'."

"What a great ruse. I might try that strategy out myself. Presumably Bob was very angry with his brother once he learned what had happened."

"He was incandescent with rage," said Pemberley. "He attacked Hector, and the pair had to be separated by the old manservant."

"Goodness! Quite the family rift, then."

"It never healed, either," Pemberley continued, "as the war began just a few days later. The brothers signed up to fight and went away, and that was that. Few tears were shed when Hector Donkin died, I'm sorry to say."

"I'm not surprised. It sounds as though he was quite an unpleasant man. What became of the princess?"

"She must of wen' back to 'er father and the princelin'," said Mrs Robertson.

"I still remember her name for some strange reason," said Pemberley. "It was quite a mouthful. Princess Wilhelmina Herzeleide Alexandrine von der Steinburg."

"Good grief!" exclaimed Churchill. "What did they call her for short?"

"I've no idea," she replied.

"An' now Bob's gone an' all!" said the cook, tears welling in her eyes.

Pemberley also began to sniff. She pushed a handkerchief up beneath her spectacles to dab at her eyes.

"Don't worry, ladies. We shall soon find the culprit," said Churchill.

"It feels like an impossible task," sobbed Pemberley. "And now that Inspector Mappin's involved we've no chance of getting close to the investigation."

"Oh, but we will. We always find a way, don't we? I'm feeling much more optimistic now that I've had something to eat. Let's head back upstairs and have a sniff about. We need to find out how the ornamental letter opener went from harmlessly opening an envelope in the vicar's hand to being ruthlessly plunged into Bob Donkin's back."

"If only ornamental letter openers could speak."

"Indeed, Pembers. That would make our job a darn sight easier, wouldn't it?"

Chapter Nine

ONCE CHURCHILL HAD POLISHED off the loaf in the kitchen, the two ladies headed back upstairs. They found Mrs Thonnings entangled in what appeared to be an argument with Miss Pauling from the orphanage outside the music room.

"Oh no," said Pemberley with a groan. "We forgot to intervene before she got to '*Keyhole in the Door*'."

"Oh dear," replied Churchill. "I hope the children aren't too upset."

"They don't even understand the words!" Mrs Thonnings protested to Miss Pauling.

"They understand more than you realise," she replied. "And they repeat them, too. I sincerely hope they don't do so when the Bishop of Sherborne visits us tomorrow."

"I don't know what all the fuss is about these days," replied Mrs Thonnings. "You should have heard the songs I was singing at their age."

"Mrs Thonnings," said Churchill brightly, "how would you like to come and help us with our case?"

"Oh, I'd love to," she replied. "I was trying to cheer the

orphans up, but it seems my efforts weren't appreciated. Shall we go and get some sherry and bitters?"

"I think you've probably had enough, Mrs Thonnings. Let's step into the drawing room."

Inspector Mappin and the vicar were already in there.

"Ah, just the ladies I need to speak to!" announced Mappin, walking over to them with his notebook in hand.

"Really?" replied Churchill. "Perhaps you're interested to hear what we've discovered so far."

"I'm more interested in your whereabouts at the time of Mr Donkin's murder, Mrs Churchill."

"Why, pray tell, would you be interested in that?"

"It's just a question we're asking everyone."

"Oh, I see. In that case the answer is quite simple. I was in this very room listening to Mr Hurricks reciting *A Christmas Carol* by the renowned author Mr Charles Dickens."

The inspector wrote this down. "Do you have a witness?"

"Why on earth would I need a witness, Inspector? You don't, for one minute, suspect that I had something to do with this crime, do you?"

"It's just a question we're asking everyone."

"Right. Well, I was sitting next to a chap who was wearing a tartan jacket. I don't know his name, but he kept knocking into me with his elbow."

"That would be Mr Fordbridge," said the vicar.

"Ah yes, him."

"And you can confirm that you were in this very room, Mrs Churchill, at the time of the murder?" asked the inspector.

"Yes. Mr Hurricks had just got to the Ghost of Christmas Yet to Come and was performing a sinister pointing gesture with his finger. It was then that we all heard the screams."

"So you were definitely here in this room at the time the murder was discovered."

"Yes."

"But where were you at the time of the murder itself?"

"Well, I don't know where I was at the time of the murder itself because I don't know exactly when it took place. The doctor seemed to think it had happened less than half an hour before we went in there, and the time then would have been…"

"We have established that the time of death was between half-past six and ten minutes to seven, when Mrs Stonecastle discovered the body."

"But you don't know the exact time of the murder?"

"No. Do you?"

"How could I?"

"You and Miss Pemberley were the last people to see Mr Donkin alive."

"No we weren't!" Churchill gave a laugh. "The murderer was the last person to see Mr Donkin alive."

"Or *murderers*."

"You think there was more than one?"

"You tell me, Mrs Churchill. The choir members exited the parlour at half-past six, and they left Mr Donkin alone with you and Miss Pemberley. The next time he was seen there was a knife sticking out of his back."

"Letter opener."

"That may be so, but it happened to be used as a lethal weapon."

"Rather over-engineered for its appointed task, isn't it? All it need do under normal circumstances is cut open a layer of paper. It's rather like cracking a nut with a sledge-hammer, if you ask me."

"I didn't ask you."

"Indeed you didn't. You seem to be asking a number of probing questions that hint, if you don't mind me saying so, at a possible involvement in the murder on the part of Miss Pemberley and myself."

"As I said before, you were the last people to see him alive, Mrs Churchill."

"Someone had to be, didn't they? Someone honest and law-abiding, that is. The real murderer is hardly likely to admit that he was the last person to see Mr Donkin alive, is he? In fact, he must have gone about the whole thing in a quiet and surreptitious manner so as not to be caught in the act."

"May I ask what passed between you and Mr Donkin after the choir left the room?"

"Miss Pemberley's dog, Oswald, had bitten his baton in two, which added to his already angry demeanour. He waved both pieces of it in my face and told me I would regret ever coming to the Vicarage Christmas Party. And he wasn't wrong on that score, to be quite honest with you."

"What happened then?"

"I asked him where he had got his mince pie from but he wouldn't tell me, so we left."

"Your statement suggests that the choirmaster was angry even before your dog bit his baton."

"Miss Pemberley's dog. And yes, he was miffed because his choir had just walked out on him."

"Why was that?"

"He was rude to them."

"I heard you scolded him for the way he spoke to them."

"I certainly did!"

"So it's safe to say that shortly before his death Mr

Donkin had been repeatedly riled by you."

"He was riled before we appeared on the scene, Inspector. He was shouting at the choir for not singing their carols properly. He was clearly a man who became riled easily, which, when you consider what happened with the Prussian princess all those years ago, is hardly surprising."

Inspector Mappin gave a frustrated groan. "You've been listening to village gossip again, I see."

"Such a sad tale, Inspector."

"If any of it's even true."

"Why wouldn't it be?"

"There was a rumour that Mr Donkin simply invented the story," said the vicar. "There was talk that he'd invented it to account for why he never married."

"Well, that could be little more than village gossip, too," retorted Churchill. "Surely his brother Hector must have mentioned the Prussian princess to someone."

"He never spoke of it," said the vicar. "He went off to war and that was the end of that."

"I suppose if it happened just before they went off, he wouldn't have had a chance to tell many people about it."

"Exactly," replied the vicar. "Very convenient, wouldn't you say?"

"I thought you liked Mr Donkin, Vicar?"

"Oh, I did. He was a thoroughly decent chap. But he was known for telling a few far-fetched stories here and there. He didn't mean anything malicious by it; he just wanted to make his life sound a little more interesting than it was."

"And what of the footprints in the snow, Vicar? Did you find any leading away from the parlour window?" asked Churchill.

"Impossible to say, I'm afraid. The freshly laid snow

was completely vandalised by the orphans. There are wonky snowmen and tiny footprints everywhere."

"Well, if the murderer did escape through the parlour window, he somehow managed to lock it from the inside and draw the curtains behind him," said Churchill. "An impossible feat, if you ask me."

"Unless he – or *she* – had an accomplice," said the inspector.

"Why would the murderer escape via the window and leave his accomplice in the house?"

Inspector Mappin considered this. "Perhaps the murderer was somehow easier to spot than the accomplice. Perhaps the accomplice was someone no one would suspect."

"I'd imagine the *murderer* is someone no one would suspect," said Churchill. "That's how they usually get away with it."

"Which brings us back to you and Miss Pemberley, Mrs Churchill."

Chapter Ten

"IT's QUITE ridiculous to suggest that Miss Pemberley and I had anything to do with the murder of the choirmaster, Inspector."

"Your argument with Mr Donkin might have escalated into a physical tussle," suggested Inspector Mappin.

Churchill gave a cynical laugh. "Absolutely not!"

"You'd disbanded his choir and your dog had bitten his baton. And he was already feeling incensed by his choir's poor performance."

"He only had himself to blame for getting so cross."

"Perhaps so, but maybe he did more than just wave the pieces of broken baton in your face. Maybe he actually poked you with them."

"Only he didn't. What a silly notion!"

"Perhaps he gave you or Miss Pemberley a little shove."

"He was angry, but I feel quite sure that he would never have laid a finger on two old ladies."

"Perhaps you were fearful and felt the need to defend yourselves."

"We were never at any time fearful, were we, Miss Pemberley? Indeed, there was nothing to be fearful of!"

"Perhaps on the spur of the moment you felt the need to protect yourselves. You saw the letter opener on the table close by, you seized it and—"

"Can I stop you there, Inspector? It's just that I've never heard so much tummy rot in all my years. Miss Pemberley and I did not murder Mr Donkin. If we had, I'd go ahead and admit it now just to get it all over and done with. You're wasting your time with this line of questioning; we need to get on and find out who the real murderer is. You mentioned the letter opener in your little piece of fiction there. How did it come to be lying on a table in the parlour, when moments before it had been safely stowed in the vicar's hand?"

"The vicar put it there."

"Did you put it there, Vicar?" Churchill asked.

"Did I put what where? Sorry, I didn't hear what you said. Mrs Thonnings was speaking to me."

"Did you put your letter opener on a table in the parlour?"

"No."

"What did you do with it after you opened the envelope and announced that Mrs Stonecastle was the winner of the Christmas cake competition?" asked Churchill.

"I'm not really sure. I would have rested it somewhere, I expect. It's a little sharp to keep in one's pocket."

"Where is it usually kept?"

"In the drawer in my study."

"Did you put it back there after opening the envelope and announcing the winner of the Christmas cake competition?"

"No. I'm certain of that because I didn't go into my

study after that. I haven't been in my study all evening, in fact."

"Then where did you leave the letter opener?"

"I'm not quite sure… Let me have a little think. I still had the envelope and the letter opener in my hand when I introduced Mr Hurricks, and then… Well, I must have just popped them down somewhere. On the mantelpiece, perhaps."

"Did you remain in this room?"

"No. I went into the music room, where I recall speaking to Mrs Thonnings beside the harp."

"I also remember you speaking to Mrs Thonnings beside the harp, Vicar," said Churchill, "and I don't believe you had the letter opener or the envelope in your hand at that point."

"Which lends credence to the theory that I had put them down somewhere."

"Indeed." Churchill felt her teeth clench with frustration. "Shall we have a look in the music room? I'd wager that the envelope is still in there."

They crossed the corridor that led to the music room, where Mr Hurricks had taken it upon himself to perform *A Christmas Carol* to the children. He scowled at the new arrivals as they entered.

"Sorry to interrupt, Mr Hurricks," said the vicar. "I was just wondering whether I left an envelope in here."

Mr Hurricks paused and placed his hands on his hips as the vicar looked around the room.

"Ah, there it is," the vicar said, picking up an envelope from the mantelpiece.

"You think you placed the murder weapon on the mantelpiece, do you?" the inspector asked the vicar.

"Murder?" one of the children cried out.

"You mean *letter opener*," interrupted Churchill.

"Is there a murderer here?" asked another child.

"No, of course not," said Miss Pauling.

"There's a weapon, though," said a girl with thick spectacles.

"No there isn't," Miss Pauling replied.

"But there is. The vicar told the policeman he put it up there."

"Children, please listen to Mr Hurricks' story instead of spouting idle gossip."

"He's boring."

"Is the murderer going to get us?" asked one child, her voice wavering.

Another burst into tears.

"Oh, good grief," exclaimed Miss Pauling. "First we had rude songs from that lady with the red hair and now there's all this talk about a murder. It's not good for the children's minds, Inspector!"

"I do apologise for the inconvenience," said Inspector Mappin, "but the fact of the matter is that a crime has been committed and we need to find the culprit before someone else gets hurt."

"Who's going to get hurt?" asked another child.

More tears followed.

"Vicar, I suggest that you hand the aforementioned envelope over to Inspector Mappin and that we take our leave," said Churchill. "Poor children. They shouldn't have to listen to this sort of thing at Christmastime."

"I'd say that Mr Donkin came off rather worse, wouldn't you, Mrs Churchill?"

"Did the vicar murder him?" asked a child. "He had a weapon, after all."

"Certainly not!" said Miss Pauling.

"Let's leave," Churchill said with greater urgency.

"I just need to check the mantelpiece first," said

Inspector Mappin. "After all, this is where the killer must have retrieved the weapon from."

"I knew it!" said the girl with thick spectacles.

"Perhaps we should all move to another room and leave the inspector to get on with his investigation," said Miss Pauling. "Mr Hurricks can continue his story there."

"Mr Hurricks smells."

"Don't be rude. Apologise at once!"

"No need to leave the room, Miss Pauling," said Inspector Mappin. "I've surveyed all that I need to survey for now."

They left the music room and returned to the drawing room.

"That settles it, then," said Churchill. "Vicar, you left the envelope and letter opener on the mantelpiece in the music room, then chatted to Mrs Thonnings beside the harp. As you did so, the murderer crept into the music room, took the letter opener from the mantelpiece and slunk off into the parlour to do the dirty deed."

"Weren't you in the music room while the vicar was talking to Mrs Thonnings beside the harp, Mrs Churchill?" asked the inspector.

"Yes, I was. As was Miss Pemberley."

"How very interesting."

"But we didn't take the letter opener, if that's what you're implying."

"Did you see anyone else take it?"

"Of course not. I'd say so otherwise, wouldn't I?"

"Hmmm." Inspector Mappin jotted down some observations in his notebook. "I think it's time for interviews now. No one must leave the vicarage until we've interviewed them thoroughly."

"If you're going to do that, Inspector, why don't you open up the morning room again so we can at least help ourselves to a little refreshment?" suggested Churchill. "You can't hold everyone here and starve them, you know. May I ask which important piece of evidence you discovered in the morning room that has forced it to be shut off?"

"It was merely a precaution, but I think we are now in a position to reopen it."

"Thank goodness for that. Ever since I got here earlier this evening... Come to think of it, it feels as though we arrived here yesterday! Doesn't it feel as though we've been trapped inside this vicarage forever, Miss Pemberley?"

"It does, rather."

"Anyway, ever since we arrived I've been looking forward to seeing the mince pie mountain. It was terribly upsetting to find that it had been shut away in the morning room."

"I should think we could allow you to indulge yourself with a few mince pies, Mrs Churchill."

"Thank you."

"You'll need to build up your reserves for all the questioning I have planned."

"Surely you're not going to question me any further, Inspector. You've already interrogated me enough!"

"I haven't even got started, Mrs Churchill. Let's be mindful that it was *you* who was the last person to see Mr Donkin alive, *you* who argued with him shortly before his death and *you* who was in the music room when the vicar left the murder weapon on the mantelpiece."

"And Miss Pemberley, Inspector. She was there, too. And if we were guilty of the crime, may I ask why we are still standing with you here rather than scarpering off through the snow?"

"To mislead me, I suppose. You chose to remain present in the hope that I wouldn't suspect you."

"What utter tosh!"

"Go and help yourself to some mince pies, Mrs Churchill, and we shall speak again in a little while."

"I can hardly wait, Inspector."

~

The morning room was duly unlocked, and Churchill made sure she was the first person to bustle in there.

"Let me at them, Pembers! Eh? Where are they? Oh dear, this doesn't look right."

Churchill and Pemberley stopped to survey the scene. Food that had once been carefully piled on plates lay scattered across the table and on the floor. Churchill stepped forward and observed an array of half-nibbled sandwiches and chewed-up pieces of cheese. The most devastating sight was that of the pastry crumbs littered across the floor as far as the eye could see. A large platter, which had presumably once supported the mince pie mountain, was empty save for a handful of sorry-looking, half-eaten mince pies.

"Good grief, Pembers! Someone's been in here!"

"Some*dog*'s been in here."

"What? A dog, you say?"

It was then that Churchill noticed a scruffy-haired form peacefully sleeping beneath the table, happily surrounded by the food detritus.

"Oh no! Is that Oswald? How on earth did he get in here? I thought you said he was lying on the vicar's bed!"

"That was just a guess. I didn't realise he was in here, though."

"Inspector Mappin must have shut him in here with all the food! Of all the slow-witted, wooden-headed, dunce-like—"

"Is there a problem, Mrs Churchill?" asked the vicar as

he walked into the room. "Oh, good grief! Whatever has happened now?"

"Good grief, indeed. Inspector Mappin shut a dog in with all the food! *Our* food! And now it's ruined!"

"*A* dog? Do you mean *your* dog?"

"*Miss Pemberley's* dog."

"Not him again! He's single-handedly created all this mess, has he? How in heaven's name did he get in here?"

"We don't know, Vicar. He was in the yard earlier, but somehow he must have found his way back into the house and got himself shut in with the food. How on earth could Inspector Mappin have shut a dog inside a room without noticing?"

"If the dog had been kept under control it never would have happened!"

"You really should keep your dog under control, Miss Pemberley!" scolded Churchill.

Pemberley's face crumpled as Churchill and the vicar glared at her.

"I do try," she whimpered, "but he's very clever."

"There's nothing very clever about eating all the party food!" said Churchill crossly.

"It's quite disgraceful," said the vicar. "We can't expect poor Mrs Robertson to make more sandwiches and mince pies at this hour. Besides, I haven't the time to ask her. I've got to go and greet the undertaker, who has just arrived with the coffin. In all my years of hosting the Vicarage Christmas Party I have never known one go as badly as this one!"

The vicar stormed out of the room, leaving Churchill and Pemberley alone.

"I suppose I'd better wake Oswald," said Pemberley, miserably.

"I'd leave him if I were you, Pembers. It's better that

he's sound asleep than biting the vicar's ankles and eating enough food for forty-five people. You know what they say about sleeping dogs."

"They snore?"

"Well, sometimes they do, I suppose. And when they're having a vivid dream they kick their legs about in rather an endearing manner, don't they? It's quite sweet, really. But that's not what the proverb says about sleeping dogs."

"Oh, I remember now. Let them lie, isn't it?"

"Absolutely. I find that the old advice is always the best. Now, I do believe there are a few salvageable mince pies among this lot. What do you think?"

Chapter Eleven

CHURCHILL AND PEMBERLEY seated themselves in a couple of easy chairs and ate the half-nibbled mince pies while Oswald continued his nap beneath the table. Every now and then someone entered the room, observed the mess, looked bewildered and left again.

"We should probably tidy some of this up, Pembers. I feel partly responsible for it, even though it's entirely Inspector Mappin's fault for locking Oswald in here."

"We've done quite a good job of eating some of the mess."

"We have, but even I'm starting to reach my limit. In the meantime, we need to come up with a few suspects before Mappin decides he's well and truly going to pin this crime on us."

"But how can he? We didn't do it!"

"You know that and I know that, but this is Mappin we're talking about. He always tries to find the easiest way out, and unfortunately we appear to have been in all the wrong places at all the wrong times as far as this murder is concerned."

"It could have been one of the choir members."

"It could indeed. How many members would you say the choir has?"

"Twenty or so."

"That sounds about right," said Churchill with a nod. "And I suppose we can discount the children."

"Why?"

"Because the culprit is hardly likely to be a child, is it?"

"It might be. Some children are horrid!"

"I think we should discount the children, which leaves us with about a dozen choir members."

"That makes for quite a number of suspects," said Pemberley.

"It certainly does. Now, who else do we have?"

"The vicar."

"An unlikely suspect, but I suppose we should consider him."

"Mrs Stonecastle."

"The winner of the Christmas cake competition?"

"Yes. She discovered the body, didn't she?" said Pemberley. "She could have done it."

"In which case she'd need to be a jolly good actress, as she appeared to be very distressed by the incident. Is she a good actress?"

"I've no idea. Mr Hurricks could also be a suspect."

"Oh no, it couldn't have been him. He started blathering on as soon as the choir left the drawing room, and he blathered on through our little to-do with Mr Donkin in the parlour, and he was still blathering on when I returned to the drawing room and had to listen to the rest of his ghosts. His booming voice provided the backdrop to the entire episode."

"Mrs Thonnings, then."

"Mrs Thonnings? Surely not. Why would she want to murder Mr Donkin?"

"I don't know. Why would anyone want to murder him?"

"Good question, but for now I think we need to concentrate on the people he had fallen out with."

"Like us, you mean?"

"No, not like us at all. One choir member who springs to mind is that chap with the wavy grey hair who said he wished he'd joined the choir at Heythrop Itching. Do you know the one I mean?"

"Ah, yes. He was quite put out, wasn't he? That's Mr Swipplekirk."

"Good. Let's add him to our list. We're going to have to question these people as soon as possible, but we'll need to do it surreptitiously. We can't have Mappin getting wind of what we're up to. What are you doing, Pembers?"

Pemberley had risen from her seat and was admiring another bookcase.

"I'm having a little peruse of the books here."

"Not again! We don't have time for reading. We've a murder to solve before we find ourselves thrown into the cells."

"Inspector Mappin wouldn't do that."

"What makes you so sure? If he decides to arrest us because he's too cack-handed to find the proper culprit there won't be a great deal we can do about it. Let's get on with it. Oh, hello Oswald."

The little dog had stirred. He got to his feet and shook himself.

"I hope you're proud of yourself for destroying the mince pie mountain. Auntie Churchy is very cross with you."

The dog stared back at her with his large brown eyes.

Churchill tried to muster her best angry expression but failed.

The little dog trotted over to Pemberley, who was still standing beside the bookcase.

"Watch this new trick he does," she said. "He's learned how to jump into my arms."

"Now is not the time for doggy tricks," replied Churchill as she brushed the crumbs from her bosom and stood to her feet. "Let's go and find Mr Swivelkick or whatever he's called."

"Jump to Mummy, Oswald!"

"Come along, Pembers."

"Jump to Mummy! Oh, he's not doing it now."

"He's eaten too much, that's why," replied Churchill as she walked toward the door. "I can't say that I'd like to do any jumping after eating a bellyful of mince pies and other sundries."

"Jump to Mummy! Oh, forget about it, then... Oof!"

A thud followed by a splintering creak made Churchill spin around. The bookcase was standing at a strange angle and Pemberley appeared to be half-embedded in the wall. Oswald gave an excitable bark.

"Good grief!" exclaimed Churchill, dashing over to the bookcase. "Pembers?"

"I'm fine," she replied, pulling herself out of the wall. The little dog had finally jumped into her arms and was licking her face. "He decided to jump up once I'd assumed he wasn't going to. It took me completely by surprise! I hadn't realised how wobbly the vicar's bookcase was."

"This is more than a wobbly bookcase, Pembers, don't you see? You've uncovered a secret passageway!"

Chapter Twelve

PEMBERLEY TURNED to examine the bookcase. It had pivoted so that one end had turned into the room and the other end angled into a dark passageway.

"Quick! Let's go inside before anyone notices!"

Pemberley took a step back. "I don't like the dark."

"It's not that dark in there, Pembers. Come on!"

"It's pitch black!"

"But we need to investigate and find out where it leads."

"Not in the dark, we don't."

"Hurry up! If someone comes into the room and sees the bookcase all lopsided like this, we'll have lost our opportunity!" Churchill felt her heart thudding impatiently at the back of her throat.

Pemberley glanced over at the fireplace. "Perhaps we could take a candle from the mantelpiece."

"Yes, right. Do it! Do it now!"

Pemberley put Oswald down and dashed over to the mantelpiece. She found a box of matches with which to light the candle in an elaborate brass candlestick, then walked carefully back with it so as not to extinguish the flame.

"Yes, yes, very good. Come along, Pembers. You lead the way with your candle."

Pemberley reached the bookcase and peered into the darkness beyond it. "Do you think there might be spiders in there?"

"Probably," replied Churchill, giving her a firm nudge in the back. "Come on, then. In we go!"

Pemberley slipped into the tunnel with Oswald following at her heels. Churchill launched herself forward and squeezed herself as hard as she could through the gap that had opened up between the bookcase and the wall. For one terrible moment she thought she might not make it through, and then, for an even worse moment, she thought she might be completely stuck. But after a deep exhalation she just managed to squeeze into the passage behind Pemberley. Then she seized the end of the bookcase and rotated it back into position.

"Perfect," she said as it fitted neatly into place. Now no one will know we're in here! Fancy this, eh, Pembers! You read about these things in old houses all the time but you never expect to find yourself inside one. How exciting!"

"I don't like it at all." The candlelight flickered against Pemberley's glum, bespectacled face. The wood-panelled passageway was only just wide enough to admit Churchill's sizeable frame. Thick cobwebs draped from the ceiling.

"I have a strange inkling, Pembers."

"About what?"

"That our murderer may have known about this secret tunnel. It might explain why he didn't leave by the parlour window."

"That theory would only work if this passageway led to the parlour."

"Exactly. Let's test it out, then, shall we? Lead on!"

The two ladies and Oswald made their way along the passage.

"Hark, Pembers!" whispered Churchill. "Do you hear that?"

They paused.

"What?" asked Pemberley.

"Voices!"

As they listened intently through the wood-panelled wall they heard a familiar booming voice.

"Mr Hurricks is off again," said Churchill. "It's as if he doesn't have anything else to do with his time at a Christmas party."

"We must be next to the music room," said Pemberley, "where he seems to be reciting *A Christmas Carol* to the orphans. Those poor children. As if they haven't suffered enough already!"

"Well, they've got the Bishop of Sherborne visiting them tomorrow. That'll cheer them up, I'm sure. Come on, let's keep going."

The passage continued for a short while longer, then stopped abruptly at a wood-panelled wall.

"What do you think, Pembers? Another bookcase?"

"It might be."

"Let's give it a little nudge and see what happens."

"But what if there's someone in the room?"

They listened carefully for a moment.

"I can't hear any voices. Let's just give this door the tiniest of nudges and see."

Pemberley pushed against the door but nothing happened.

"You'll need to put your back into it, Pembers. Let me hold the candle while you give it another go."

Pemberley pushed again but the door still didn't budge.

"Crikey, Pembers! How did the murderer get through here?"

"Perhaps he didn't."

She gave the door another hefty shove and it suddenly swung open on one side. The end of the bookcase careered into the passageway and the two ladies leapt back out of its way just in time.

Chapter Thirteen

THERE WAS SILENCE FOR A MOMENT. Churchill held her breath, terrified that someone might have seen the bookcase move.

When no sound came, they peered cautiously into the room. A smile spread across Churchill's face when she saw that they were standing in the empty parlour.

"It's just as we thought, Pembers!"

Oswald ran into the room and sniffed around. The fire had almost completely burned down in the grate and the room was half-dark. The candle provided a little more light, revealing an outline of chalk on the oriental rug where Mr Donkin's body had lain.

"The undertaker has removed the body, then," said Churchill. "One could never imagine when attending a party the possibility that one might leave it in a coffin."

"Oh gosh, no one ever would!" replied Pemberley, her voice cracking. "And now the idea's been dropped into my mind I shall think it whenever I go to one. I shan't ever go to a party again!"

"Don't allow Mr Donkin's tragic demise to put you off,

Pemberley. Women like us need to get out and enjoy ourselves while we still have the chance." She handed the candle back to her assistant. "Now, I don't think we need to stay in this room any longer, seeing as we've established that the secret passageway leads to the parlour, and there's a danger that Mappin will come in again and find us here. Come on, Pembers, we've made magnificent progress! Let's get back before anyone realises what we've discovered."

Pemberley stepped into the passageway with the candle with Oswald in pursuit. Churchill squeezed herself back in before closing the bookcase door behind her.

"Oh, how I hate cobwebs!" hissed Pemberley, rubbing at her head. "There are so many in my hair I'm no longer sure what's hair and what's cobweb!"

"A nice shampoo and set will sort that out, Pembers. If we ever get out of this blasted vicarage, that is."

They reached the morning room bookcase door and paused to listen for voices. Sure enough, they could hear talking on the other side. The two ladies glanced at each other, wide-eyed in the candlelight, making an unspoken pact to remain silent. They glanced down at the little dog, praying that he wouldn't bark and give them away. He looked up at them as if he had no intention of doing such a thing, the candlelight reflecting in his large brown eyes.

"What a dreadful mess," said a voice that Churchill instantly recognised as Inspector Mappin's.

"It was that dog, you know the one," replied the vicar. "That ragged, feral thing owned by those two old detective ladies."

"Ah, yes. Mrs Churchill and Miss Pemberley."

"With a bit of luck they've cleared off home with it by now."

"I hope not; they're my prime suspects! If you

remember rightly, Vicar, I asked everyone to remain in the vicarage while I conducted my interviews. If they've scarpered we can only assume that they're guilty."

"Do you really think they could have done it, Inspector? Two elderly ladies? I realise the large one's a pain in the posterior, but a *murderess*?"

"The idea seems a little far-fetched, I grant you that. But the murderer must be one of your party guests, and therefore he or she is bound to appear rather unlike a murderer. After all, you wouldn't have invited someone who looked like a murderer to the Vicarage Christmas Party, would you?"

"Absolutely not. I only invited the great and good of the village, or so I thought."

"Quite! Myself included, of course, though I couldn't attend because I was on duty."

"Indeed. But as it turns out you made it here anyway."

"So I did."

"I struggle to comprehend how you can invite the great and good to a party and still end up with a murderer in your midst."

"I'm afraid it's the way of the world these days, Vicar. And my money's on Mrs Churchill, with the likely assistance of Miss Pemberley."

The two ladies stared at each other in the gloom, open-mouthed.

"They were the last two to see Donkin alive," continued the inspector, "and the choir members tell me that angry words were exchanged just before they left the parlour."

"But how did they get hold of the ornamental letter opener?"

"One of them, Mrs Churchill probably, must have swiped it off the mantelpiece in the music room and secreted it in her handbag. You saw her in the music room, didn't you?"

"Yes. Miss Pemberley was there, too."

"And no one would have batted an eyelid upon seeing an old lady with an ornamental letter opener. It didn't become a weapon until it was plunged into Mr Donkin's back, did it? Until that point it was nothing but a harmless piece of stationery. She made a clever choice when it came to the murder weapon."

"You really think it was Mrs Churchill, Inspector?"

"Who else could it have been?"

"Have you dusted the letter opener for fingerprints?"

"Not yet. I'm still waiting for it to be removed from Mr Donkin's back at the moment. I expect the police surgeon will do that down at the mortuary. The only trouble with dusting for fingerprints, Vicar, is that yours will also be on the letter opener."

"Of course they will; I use it every day to open my post. I shall miss the darn thing, actually, as it was an extremely useful letter opener. My housekeeper's prints will be on it as well, I expect. But even if you find Mrs Churchill's fingerprints on it you'll be a bit stuck, because it doesn't necessarily follow that she's the murderer."

"Ah, but it does."

"How can that be if it also has my and the housekeeper's fingerprints on it?"

"Because your fingerprints and those of your housekeeper would be on the weapon for a reason. The only reason Mrs Churchill had to pick that letter opener up was to use it as a weapon."

"But we can't be sure of that. She may have picked it up from the mantelpiece, considering it an attractive letter opener – which it was – admired it, then placed it back down."

"I can't imagine her doing so."

"But you can't rule it out, Inspector. In fact, Miss Pemberley or just about any other guest at the party this evening may have done the same thing. Fingerprints on the weapon do not a culprit make. The murderer's prints may not be on the weapon at all if he chose to wear gloves. Gloves would have been a sensible choice if he had planned the murder in advance."

Inspector Mappin sighed. "Why did you ask if the weapon had been dusted for fingerprints, Vicar, if you're so determined to disregard any that may be found there?"

"That's a good point. I've sort of talked it out of relevance, haven't I? Though I suppose the fingerprint evidence could prove useful when coupled with other findings."

"Such as what?"

"Such as a witness noticing the murderer entering or leaving the crime scene."

"That would be useful evidence indeed. If only we could find such a witness!"

"I'm sure you will. I must say, I've quite enjoyed discussing the details of the case in this manner. Do you know what, Inspector? I think I'd make quite a good detective!"

Inspector Mappin groaned again. "You have no idea how many times I've heard people say that."

"Ah, hello Mrs Grunchen. You're here to tidy up, I see," said the vicar. "And not before time."

"What's 'appened 'ere?" queried a lady's voice.

"Some beastly little animal got in and ransacked the place, as you can see."

"Were it a rat?"

"No, a dog, in actual fact. A sort of rat dog."

Pemberley gave a snort of indignation, but Churchill urged her to remain quiet with a fearful grimace.

"I'll tell you what, Inspector, I might just have a sit down here and watch Mrs Grunchen tidy up," said the vicar. The squeak of chair springs stretching beneath his weight followed. "It's been an odd sort of an evening. Very odd indeed, I'd say. I could do with a rest."

"I shall go and make further enquiries," replied Inspector Mappin. "Would you please send Mrs Churchill and Miss Pemberley my way if you happen to see them?"

"Of course, Inspector. You've missed a piece of mince pie crust under the chaise lounge, Mrs Grunchen. Can you see it tucked under there?"

Chapter Fourteen

"Oh, MARVELLOUS!" whispered Pemberley. "Now we're stuck in here while the vicar watches Mrs Grunchen tidy up."

"I'm sure it won't take her long, Pembers."

"I bet it will. It could take a whole hour! And we'll be done for if Oswald decides he's had enough and starts barking."

"Perhaps we could leave him in the parlour."

"He'll most likely destroy important evidence around the murder scene if we do."

"That's a fair point. Well, he's been pretty good so far. Hopefully the vicar and Mrs Grunchen will leave soon."

"Only they won't, will they? You've seen the mess Mrs Grunchen has to tidy up. It could take her all night!"

"Come now, Pembers, you're exaggerating."

"I hate dark, enclosed spaces."

"We have a candle to light the way."

"But it won't last forever, will it?"

"We won't be here forever."

"I say, Mrs Grunchen," came the vicar's voice from the other side of the bookcase. "I don't suppose you know where the other candlestick's gone, do you?"

The two ladies in the passageway froze.

"Which one's that, then, Vicar?" asked Mrs Grunchen.

"One of the pair that sits on the mantelpiece. There are usually two of them, but now there's only one."

"Praps someone's tooken one of 'em."

"I'd say so, wouldn't you? Any idea who?"

"I never even noticed one of 'em was missin', Vicar."

"I hope no one's stolen it. They're quite valuable, you know. They were gifted to one of my predecessors by the Bishop of Sherborne. Bronze, as you can see, and quite noted for their attractive faceted shafts. Oh, I really hope no one's stolen it. Or... Good grief, no. Surely that's not possible!"

"What ain't impossible?"

"*Not possible*, I said. No, no, no!"

The chair springs creaked again as the vicar apparently rose from his seat.

"What's botherin' you, Vicar?"

"I can't help but recall the moment when I was discussing poor Mr Donkin's murder with my guests. People began suggesting various other murder weapons, such as lead piping and candlesticks. I warned them they might be giving the murderer ideas, and now it seems they have! The murderer has purloined one of my prized candlesticks and is most likely stalking the corridors with it as we speak!"

A loud shriek emerged from Mrs Grunchen.

"Calm down, my good woman. I'll fetch the inspector and get him to see to all this. We'll catch that murderer. By Jove, we will!"

Still standing nervously in the dingy secret passage, the two ladies glanced at the candlestick in Pemberley's hand.

"I can see what he means by the faceted shaft," whispered Pemberley as she inspected it closely. "It really is quite attractive, isn't it?"

"You'll need to wipe your fingerprints off when we're done with it, Pembers. We don't want to implicate ourselves any further in this gruesome affair."

"The vicar appears to have left the room," whispered Pemberley. "Do you think Mrs Grunchen's still in there?"

"I think so. I can hear tidying-up noises."

"Do you think we could creep out of here and swear her to secrecy?"

"Absolutely not. We've never met her before, and we have no idea whether we can trust her to keep the fact that we've found the secret passageway quiet."

"Do you think she even knows about it?" said Pemberley.

"Perhaps not, and she would almost certainly scream the vicarage down if we suddenly emerged from behind the bookcase."

"With a possible murder weapon in our hands!"

"Absolutely," replied Churchill. "Mappin wouldn't hesitate for a moment to throw us into the cells."

"Do you think the vicar knows about this passageway?"

"He hasn't mentioned it, has he?"

"Perhaps he likes to keep it a secret."

"That's what helps to keep secret passageways secret, I suppose. They would just be ordinary passageways if everyone talked about them, wouldn't they?"

"I think they're wonderful things until you come to be stuck inside one."

"Patience, Pembers. I expect Mrs Grunchen will take

herself off for a cup of tea shortly, and then we'll be able to sidle out."

"Our disappearance will only serve to make us seem more suspicious. You heard what Inspector Mappin said about us."

"Yes, but it merely goes to show how clueless he is. Imagine how much progress could be made if he concentrated on catching the real culprit."

Oswald gave a loud bark, which startled Churchill to such an extent that she felt her feet momentarily leave the floor.

The two ladies stared at each other, wide-eyed and in terrified silence. The tidying-up noises on the other side of the bookcase also seemed to pause.

Churchill glared down at Oswald. "Silence!" she hissed. "Naughty doggy!"

He gave another bark in reply, which sent her heart pounding.

"We've got to get him out of here," whispered Pemberley. "He'll give us away."

"Take him down to the other end of the passageway," replied Churchill. "He's less likely to draw attention to us down there."

"I would, but I can't get past."

"Get past what?"

"You, Mrs Churchill."

Churchill looked down at her broad frame and observed that it filled the full width of the passageway.

"How about if I turn like this?" She pushed her back up against the wall, which created a small gap in front of her.

"I still don't think I'll fit through."

"I can breathe in."

Pemberley shook her head. "I'm not convinced there's enough room."

"Oh, come on, Pembers. You're little more than skin and bone! You can get through there."

"I really don't think I can."

Churchill pressed her back up against the wall as firmly as she knew how.

"Right, I'm going to breathe in as deeply as I can. Off you go, Pembers, before that mutt barks again and gives us away."

Pemberley pushed her back against the opposite wall and attempted to squeeze past Churchill's rotund stomach. She held the candlestick above their heads as she did so, causing several drops of wax to fall onto the twinset that covered Churchill's ample bosom.

"Oh, goodness! I am sorry, Mrs Churchill."

"Just get on with it. You're almost halfway there."

Pemberley made another attempt to push past and Churchill diligently held her breath, willing her stomach to hold itself in.

As more wax dropped down, Pemberley sighed and drew back to her starting position. "I'm sorry, Mrs Churchill, I can't do it. I think we'll need to go to the other end of the passageway."

"Oh goodness, really? What a palaver."

"The only alternative would be to find out whether the morning room is empty now."

"Right, let's do that, then. Oh, look! Oswald's down the other end now anyway."

The little dog had pushed through their legs and wandered off down the passageway. Churchill and Pemberley edged their way toward the back of the morning room bookcase and listened carefully.

"I can't hear a thing in there now," whispered Pemberley.

"Me neither. I wonder if Oswald's bark prompted Mrs Grunchen to investigate where the noise had come from."

"It may have done."

"Let's try nudging the bookcase open and take a look."

Slowly and carefully, the two ladies pushed one side of the bookcase until a thin strip of light appeared. They took turns to peer through.

"Looks like the coast is clear, Pembers. What do you think?"

"Yes, I think it is."

They pushed the edge of the bookcase open a little further and Churchill felt relieved to find the room empty.

"Right, we need to tiptoe out quickly and get this book-case closed again. Are you ready?"

"Ready!"

With one firm push the bookcase swung open and the two old ladies staggered out of the passageway and into the room. Oswald followed them excitedly, and Churchill pushed the bookcase back into position with a sigh of relief.

"Now, wipe your fingerprints off that candlestick, Pembers, and let's get it back up on the mantelpiece."

"What shall I wipe it with?"

"Your cardigan, of course. Speaking of cardigans, I've been meaning to ask what colour it once was."

"Cinnamon brown, but it's faded a little."

"It calls to mind the colour of muddy snow. I suppose it's quite appropriate for the current season."

Churchill extinguished the candle flame and picked the pieces of melted wax off her twinset as Pemberley wiped the candlestick clean.

"Marvellous," said Churchill, smoothing her hair. "We

did it, Pembers! No one even realised we were in there! Give me that candlestick and I'll put it back up on the mantelpiece." She pulled her own cardigan sleeve over her hand, so as not to leave any fresh fingerprints, then walked over to the fireplace with it. "The vicar will think he's going mad when he sees it back here. He'll begin to doubt whether it was ever really missing."

"Caught in the act!" came a voice just as Churchill reached up toward the mantelpiece.

Chapter Fifteen

UNBEKNOWN TO CHURCHILL, the vicar and inspector had arrived back in the morning room.

"There's your murderer!" shouted the vicar, pointing at her. "Caught red-handed with the new murder weapon!"

"I beg your pardon," she retorted. "I was just popping the candlestick back on the mantelpiece. What on earth makes you think this is a murder weapon?"

"Because you seem to favour everyday items that are capable of inflicting great harm on innocent people! And look at the way you're holding it. You're trying to avoid leaving any fingerprints on it!"

"Purely to save your staff from having to polish it, Vicar. I'm sure you know how easily antique brass marks."

"If it's not an intended murder weapon, Mrs Churchill," said Inspector Mappin, "then what on earth are you doing with it?"

"Placing it back on the mantelpiece, Inspector."

"Why was it off the mantelpiece in the first place?"

"We borrowed it, didn't we, Miss Pemberley?"

"To do what?"

"To find our way to the little girls' room, if you must ask. The lighting in this vicarage is terribly dim. At least, we find it to be so at our age."

"That's where you've been, is it?" asked the inspector. "In the bathroom?"

"Yes. We hadn't found the opportunity to spend a penny since we arrived at the party, and needs must, you know."

Inspector Mappin opened his notebook and jotted down some more notes.

"Surely you're not writing about our bathroom visit, Inspector. It's rather an embarrassment having to discuss the matter with you at all."

"I don't think any lady should be forced to discuss her bathroom visits," added Pemberley.

"Indeed not," said Churchill.

"What have you done with Mrs Grunchen?" asked the vicar.

"Well, we haven't murdered her if that's what you're implying, Vicar," Churchill replied. "In fact, we don't even know who she is."

"She's one of the ladies what does. Didn't you see her in here?"

"There was no one in here when Miss Pemberley and I returned from the bathroom. I was simply placing the candlestick back in its rightful place when all this hulla-balloo broke out."

"Mrs Grunchen was supposed to be tidying up all the mess your dog made," replied the vicar.

"Miss Pemberley and I can set about tidying up. I see that someone's already made a start; presumably your Mrs Grunchen."

"Your offer to tidy up is a helpful one, Mrs Churchill," said Inspector Mappin. "You ought to be doing something that'll keep you out of trouble, and I shall need you to remain in the vicarage while I continue with my investigation."

"How is your investigation going, Inspector?"

"Very well, thank you."

"Any suspects?"

"One or two at this stage, but I'm not at liberty to disclose anything further."

"Oh, you do enjoy being very mysterious, don't you?"

"There's no mystery, Mrs Churchill. Just the relentless grind of investigating a murder case."

"Well, you certainly sound like a man who enjoys his work."

"I do on occasion. Now, don't you go poking your nose into anything while I go about my work. Any attempt to involve yourself in this investigation will make you appear even more suspicious than you already do."

"Goodness! How you taunt me, Inspector!"

"No meddling!"

"I never meddle. I simply solve cases."

"There's no doubt that you've had luck on your side a few times, Mrs Churchill."

"Luck? I think you'll find it comes down to my advanced detective skills. But if you don't want us to help you with this tricky case that's fine. We shall set about tidying the morning room instead."

～

Churchill and Pemberley picked up some of the food from the floor and began to stack plates once the inspector and the vicar had left.

"Good boy, Oswald," said Pemberley as he nibbled at a

hock of ham. "The more of this you can eat, the less we'll have to tidy."

"We need to resume our investigations forthwith, Pembers," said Churchill.

"Won't that annoy Inspector Mappin?"

"Of course it will, but everything we do annoys him anyway. We need to find out who the culprit is, and I think we should start with the choir."

"Because they hated him the most?"

"Yes."

"There were quite a lot of them, though."

"Ah, but I've thought of a way to narrow it down. If we can find a choir member who knows about the secret passageway, we may just have found ourselves a murderer."

"But is the murderer likely to admit that he knows about the passageway?"

"He may do, if we can make our enquiries in a sort of off-guard, off-the-cuff manner. This is where the really clever questioning techniques come in."

"Oh, I'm not sure I'd be any good at those."

"You leave the questioning to me, Pembers. Detective Chief Inspector Churchill regularly explained his sophisticated interviewing technique to me. There's quite an art to it, as you can probably imagine."

"But how can we be sure that the murderer even knows about the secret passageway?"

"Because how else did he get to and from the scene of the crime? You heard what the inspector said; he can't find any witnesses. That suggests to me that the murderer entered the room surreptitiously."

"Via the passageway."

"Exactly."

"Who we got 'ere, then?" came a voice from behind them.

They turned to see a stocky lady with blue-rinsed hair and a grubby apron.

"Oh, hello. We're—"

"You shouldn't be doin' no tidyin' up. That's my job!"

"You're not Mrs Grunchen by any chance, are you?"

"Aye that'd be me. Now off yer go. I'm tidyin' up 'ere."

"We'll give you a hand, as agreed with the vicar. Besides, it was our dog who made the mess in the first place."

"I won't hear nuthin' of it. You're guests, ain't you? Now buzz off!"

"Well, if you insist."

"I does. Is that the dog what's made all the mess?"

"Yes, that's Oswald. He'd say that he was terribly sorry if he could."

"He don't look like a dog what's sorry. Now, go on and 'op it, all of yer. Out yer go!"

"We're only too happy to oblige, Mrs Grunchen. Cheerio!"

Chapter Sixteen

"It's excellent news that Mrs Grunchen has relieved us of our duties, Pembers. Now we can get on with the task at hand. What's that choir chap's name? Mr Swipe? Mr Swivel?"

"Mr Swipplekirk."

"Jolly good. Let's go and find him."

Mr Hurricks finally appeared to have stopped reciting *A Christmas Carol* in the music room, and the children were happily playing a game of charades as the two ladies walked past.

Most of the choir members were sitting around in the drawing room, talking in hushed tones and sipping tea.

Churchill spotted the wavy-haired Mr Swipplekirk talking to the tartan-jacketed Mr Fordbridge by the window. She extended her sympathies to a few members of the choir as she and Pemberley made their way through the room.

Churchill reached the window and made the pretence of parting the curtains to look out and study the snowfall.

"It's extremely snowy out there," she stated, unable to

see much out in the darkness. "Very snowy indeed. Oh, hello. It's Mr Swipplekirk, isn't it?"

"That's right," he said with a nod.

"Please accept my most sincere condolences on the sad parting of your choirmaster. It wasn't long ago that we all stood in this very room with him."

"Just two hours ago, in fact."

"It's an awful shock, isn't it?"

"Terrible."

Mr Fordbridge drained his cup of tea and wandered off to the sideboard for a refill.

"Did you know Mr Donkin well?" Churchill asked Mr Swipplekirk.

"Not especially. I've only been living in the village for around three years, you see. He was the choirmaster for about eight, apparently, and I heard that he worked at the post office for a long time before that."

"Can you think of a reason why anyone would wish to harm him?"

"Not really. He had a bit of a temper, as you saw for yourself, but that's no reason to kill someone, is it?"

"Most of us would be dead by now if it were!" laughed Churchill.

"Very true."

"He hadn't had a falling out with anyone recently, had he?"

"There was a long-standing feud with Mr Hurricks, but that related to a boundary wall issue between Mr Donkin's garden and the garden of Mr Hurricks's mother."

"How bitter was the feud?"

"Oh, quite bitter, I'd say, but then feuds always are, aren't they?"

"Did the two men ever come to blows?"

He gave a laugh. "Goodness me, no! I don't believe

either chap is the fighting kind. Or *was*, in Mr Donkin's case."

"What seems rather baffling is that no one appears to have seen the murderer entering or leaving the parlour."

"It's very odd, isn't it? I heard on the grapevine that you and Miss Pemberley were the last two to see Donkin alive."

"I expect Inspector Mappin told you that, did he?"

"Yes, he did. No one passed you in the corridor after you left the parlour, did they?"

"No. No one at all."

"Inspector Mappin thinks there was a twenty-minute window of opportunity," said Mr Swipplekirk.

"Yes, we heard that. Between half-past six and ten minutes to seven, he says."

"So between the time of you leaving Mr Donkin and Mrs Stonecastle finding him, someone must have gone into the parlour and murdered him."

"That sums it up all right," said Churchill. "Do you think it possible that a member of the choir might have returned to the parlour and done the deed?"

"Absolutely not!"

"He was very cross with you all. Perhaps someone felt mortally offended and decided to wreak his revenge on Mr Donkin with the vicar's letter opener."

"I think we were all rather fed up when he scolded us, and I shall freely admit, Mrs Churchill, that I left that room feeling very angry indeed. I think I even muttered something about wishing I'd joined the choir at Heythrop Itching, and that was quite a scandalous thing to say, seeing as they're our arch-rivals."

"But you weren't angry enough to attack the man, were you?"

"Of course not! Never in my life have I felt angry enough to plunge a dagger into someone's back!"

The room had fallen quiet by this stage and all faces turned in Mr Swipplekirk's direction.

He gave a self-conscious cough.

"No one would, would they, Mrs Churchill?" he said, lowering his voice. "Not unless he were a madman of some sort. That's what this sort of thing takes, you know, a *madman*. I really would prefer to leave the subject alone now. There's only so much speculation any of us can tolerate. We must leave the investigation in the capable hands of our local constabulary."

"Indeed," replied Churchill, trying her best to cover up a snort of derision in relation to this last remark. "It really is a mystery. Let's hope the culprit is caught soon enough, eh? In the meantime, I suppose we'll simply have to sit it out while Inspector Mappin and his men get round to questioning everyone."

She glanced around the room, taking in the ornate plasterwork on the ceiling and the polished wainscoting. "Rather a lovely old building, this vicarage, isn't it?"

"I suppose it is."

"Where do you place it? Early nineteenth century, perhaps?"

"I would imagine so. I hadn't given it a great deal of thought, if truth be told."

"I love an old building. We were talking about this earlier, weren't we, Miss Pemberley?"

"Were we?"

"Yes, you remember. We were saying something along the lines of how marvellous these old buildings are with their multitude of rooms and mysterious attics, and no doubt a secret passageway or two! Makes you wonder what secrets the vicarage holds, doesn't it, Mr Swipplekirk?"

"I don't know whether it's hiding anything as such, but I do believe there's a secret passageway around here somewhere."

Churchill gave a start. "Is there?" She turned to give Pemberley a knowing glance. "Well, I never would have thought it. Do you have any idea where it might be?"

"I think it connects a few of the rooms, though I couldn't tell you which."

"How interesting, Mr Swipplekirk. Very interesting indeed. I think we'd better go and see what Oswald's up to, Miss Pemberley."

"Oswald?" queried Mr Swipplekirk. "I don't believe I've met the man."

"He's our dog."

"Oh, I know *him*. The one that makes the vicar curse, you mean?"

"Yes, him. We'd better go and make sure he's not upsetting anyone."

Churchill hurriedly left the drawing room with Pemberley close behind.

"Why are you worried about Oswald all of a sudden, Mrs Churchill? Didn't you want to get more information out of Mr Swipplekirk?"

"We have all we need, Pembers," replied Churchill with a whisper and a grin. "He knows about the secret passageway! Didn't we say earlier that the murderer would know about the secret passageway? It's the only explanation we have as to how he got into and out of the parlour without being seen."

"Goodness! Then Mr Swipplekirk must have done it!"

"After being admonished by Mr Donkin and stating that he wished he'd joined another choir, he seized the letter opener from the mantelpiece in the music room and made his way toward the parlour via the secret passageway."

"Perhaps someone saw him entering it from the morning room."

"If we can find a witness who saw him sneaking in behind that bookcase the case will be solved, Pembers."

"Unlikely though, I'd say. He would hardly have moved the bookcase with someone else in the room, would he? He'd have waited for the coast to be clear, just as we did when we investigated the secret passageway."

"That's a good point. But someone may have seen him loitering in there, waiting for the room to empty."

"Yes. That would be interesting to find out."

"So we're looking for someone who may have seen Mr Swipplekirk hanging around in the morning room with a letter opener in his hand. Once we've found such a person we can go ahead and break the news to Mappin. He'll be rather annoyed that we've solved this case before him!"

"But if he is the murderer, why would he admit to knowing about the secret passageway? Surely the real murderer would keep quiet about it."

"Ah, but this is where my clever questioning came into play, Pembers. Did you notice how I encouraged him to talk about the passageway? I changed the subject completely so that he thought we were discussing the secrets of old buildings. It never occurred to him that his knowledge of the passageway would be relevant to the murder of Mr Donkin."

"Oh, I see."

"Now then, we need to find someone who saw Mr Swipplekirk loitering in the morning room before he carried out the dreadful deed."

The two ladies passed the library, where a group of ladies stood chatting.

"Mrs Stonecastle is in there," whispered Pemberley. "Don't you think we should talk to her? She was the person who discovered the murder, so she has to be a suspect too, don't you think?"

"Before Mr Swipplekirk's recent admission I would have said yes, Pembers, but now that we're quite sure he committed the crime I don't think Mrs Stonecastle can be considered a suspect. That said, there's no harm in speaking to her, is there?"

Chapter Seventeen

CHURCHILL AND PEMBERLEY entered the library and greeted the ladies, who were seated on a small sofa and the armchairs either side of it. Mrs Stonecastle and Mrs Thonnings were deep in conversation with the old lady in the Christmas hat and the lady with the scarlet lipstick and buck teeth.

"How are you, Mrs Stonecastle?" asked Churchill.

"She's bearing up," replied Mrs Thonnings.

"It must have been a terrible shock for you."

"Awful," agreed Mrs Thonnings. "I don't think I would ever recover if I'd found a man sprawled on the ground face down and with a dagger in his back."

"Letter opener," corrected Pemberley.

"A dagger-shaped letter opener," replied Mrs Thonnings. "The vicar really shouldn't leave such perilous items lying around."

"The vicar couldn't possibly have predicted that some miscreant would cause all this mischief with it," replied Churchill. "Can you think why someone might have borne the choirmaster master such ill will?"

"I've no idea at all," said Mrs Thonnings. "He was such a lovely man."

"He had quite a temper, as I understand it."

"Well yes, but don't we all?"

"His temper may have particularly angered someone. We witnessed him talking angrily to the members of his choir, and apparently there was an ongoing dispute with Mr Hurricks's mother about a garden wall."

"Oh dear, yes. That's a dreadful thing. She's put barbed wire on top of it now."

"It looks most unseemly," added the old lady in the Christmas hat.

"But Mr Hurricks's mother isn't here. She couldn't be, seeing as she's bedridden," said Mrs Thonnings.

"How did she put barbed wire on top of the wall, then?" asked Churchill.

"I don't know. She probably had a man do it."

"Her son, Mr Hurricks?"

"Yes, I suppose she might have asked him."

"What's your view, Mrs Stonecastle?" Churchill asked. "Did you know of anyone who might have had a personal vendetta against Mr Donkin?"

"She's still too upset to speak, poor thing," replied Mrs Thonnings. "I've reassured her that this sort of thing doesn't happen at every Vicarage Christmas Party!"

"That reassures me, too," replied Churchill. "I suspect Mr Donkin may have angered someone in the choir. What do you think, Mrs Stonecastle?"

"It's possible isn't it?" replied Mrs Thonnings. "I heard that he spoke to them quite rudely once they'd finished singing."

"Mrs Thonnings, can we please hear what Mrs Stonecastle thinks?" asked Churchill. "As the person who discovered the body, I'm quite interested in what she has to say."

"Well—"

"Mrs Thonnings!"

"Yes?"

"Please."

"Oh, I see." Mrs Thonnings sat back in her chair and folded her arms.

Mrs Stonecastle cleared her throat. "I haven't had much of a chance to gather my thoughts to be honest with you, Mrs Churchill. One moment I was excited to be winning the Christmas cake competition, and then the next I found... Oh, it was dreadful!"

"Indeed it was, Mrs Stonecastle. You have my deepest sympathies. Do you think a member of the choir could have done the deed?"

"I'm afraid I have no idea who did it, Mrs Churchill."

"But it's most likely to have been a member of the choir. Someone who was more angered by Donkin's scolding than anyone else, perhaps."

"I really don't know. I can't imagine anyone in the choir doing such a thing. I haven't been a member for terribly long, but they're such a lovely group of people... And we all get along so well together."

"Perhaps it was like the assassination of Julius Caesar," suggested Mrs Thonnings.

"What do you mean?" asked Churchill.

"Perhaps the whole choir conspired to do away with the man and set upon him with knives."

"But there was only one knife, Mrs Thonnings."

"And it was a letter opener at that," corrected Pemberley.

"Perhaps they shared it between them."

"To my knowledge there was only one wound."

"Maybe they took it out and put it back..." She winced.

"I recall Atkins had a case like that once," said Pemberley.

"The members of our choir would never do such a thing!" protested Mrs Stonecastle.

"It's a rather macabre thing to consider, Mrs Thonnings," added Churchill. "Now, Miss Pemberley and I were supposedly the last people to see Mr Donkin alive, and you, Mrs Stonecastle, were the first person to discover him dead. At some point between our respective visits to the parlour the murderer went in there and carried out his dastardly act. Don't you think it odd that no one else was seen entering or leaving the parlour?"

"It's very odd," replied Mrs Stonecastle. "You'd have thought that someone would have seen something. After all, the party was in full swing at the time."

"I'm not sure that it was exactly in '*full swing*', as you describe it, but the party was well underway, as you rightly suggest. It's extremely baffling that not a single one of the guests saw anything suspicious."

"Someone might be covering up for someone else," said Mrs Thonnings.

"That's certainly something we should consider."

"Oh good. See, I made a helpful suggestion!"

"The murderer may not have been seen because he might have made use of the secret passageway," said Mrs Stonecastle.

Churchill became speechless for a moment, her jaw slack.

"A, er... A secret passageway, Mrs Stonecastle?" she stuttered.

"Yes, it sounds rather silly really, doesn't it? But there's one that leads to the parlour, I believe."

"Right... Well, yes. The murderer may well have made

use of it, in that case. It makes sense that he did so in order to avoid being seen coming or going. Do you know much about this secret passageway, Mrs Thonnings?"

"I'd heard a rumour about a secret passageway here at the vicarage, and I must say that it's rather nice to have it confirmed. Do you know where to find it, Mrs Stonecastle?"

"I'm afraid not, although one entrance must be in the parlour, so once we're allowed in there again – not that I have any desire to ever visit that room again – you could have a good look for it."

"Very interesting," mused Churchill, feeling a strong sense of deflation. "I think we should go and look for Oswald, Miss Pemberley. We were supposed to be finding him, remember?"

"Oh yes, I remember."

"Good. Thank you for your time, ladies. Let's hope this murdering scoundrel is caught soon, eh?"

"I should think he would be," replied Mrs Thonnings. "Inspector Mappin will see to that!"

∾

"Did you just hear what I heard, Pembers?" whispered Churchill as soon as they were out of the library. "Mrs Stonecastle knows about the secret passageway. Either that means she's the murderer or more people know about it than we realised!"

"Well, you know my thoughts on the matter. I still maintain that the murderer would never admit to having any knowledge of the secret passageway," said Pemberley.

"Unless Mrs Stonecastle is bluffing."

"She's telling us she knows about it so that we'll assume she's not the murderer, you mean?"

"Yes."

"Then where does that leave Mr Swipplekirk? You thought he was the culprit because he knew about the passageway, but Mrs Stonecastle knows about it as well, and even Mrs Thonnings had heard the rumours."

"Oh, darn it, Pembers. I think my theory about Mr Swipplekirk is dead in the water before it even had a chance to sail anywhere."

"Unless Mr Swipplekirk and Mrs Stonecastle were in on it together."

"A thought that shouldn't be completely ruled out, my amiable assistant."

"They're both members of the choir, after all, and they were the most outspoken members when Mr Donkin admonished them."

"You're quite right. I think Mrs Stonecastle was cheering '*Hear, hear*' or something of the sort."

"She was indeed."

"This all makes perfect sense, Pembers. They both knew about the secret passageway, and one of them could have kept a lookout while the other used the passageway to commit the terrible crime."

"In that case, perhaps we need to find a witness who saw the pair of them loitering in the morning room."

"We could do, though I'm beginning to wonder whether our entire theory is built on rather shaky foundations. I don't think we can discount it completely, but I think we must also be open to considering other possibilities."

"Start all over again, you mean?"

"Unfortunately, yes."

"What are you two ladies doing hanging around in the corridor?" came a gruff voice.

Churchill gave a sigh as she saw the brown-whiskered Inspector Mappin glaring at them.

"I thought you were tidying up the morning room," he added.

"We were, Inspector, but Mrs Grunchen let us go."

"You didn't help her clean up?"

"We tried, really we did, but she wouldn't hear of it. I often think it's a class thing with these women, don't you? They take such great pride in their work."

"What exactly are you doing, then?"

"We're just trying to entertain ourselves for as long as we're indefinitely detained in this vicarage, Inspector. Are you asking everyone else exactly what they're *doing*? What about Mrs Thonnings? I haven't noticed you asking her what she's doing."

"No one else claims to be a private detective, Mrs Churchill."

"If you really wanted to use your time wisely, you'd ask us to assist you. We glean a lot of useful information just by-the-by, you see."

"Such as?"

"We'll tell you once you've politely asked for our assistance."

"I've a lot to be getting on with, Mrs Churchill. Rest assured that I shall be conducting an in-depth interview with you in due course."

"I'm thoroughly looking forward to it, Inspector."

Chapter Eighteen

"Darn it, Pembers!" hissed Churchill as Inspector Mappin walked away, examining his notebook as he went. "I can feel the noose tightening!"

"Goodness! Really?"

"Yes! That foolhardy inspector's gathering as much evidence against us as he possibly can, and then we'll be in for it. I need to ensure that my alibi won't let me down."

"Who's your alibi?"

"That chap in the tartan jacket. What's his name again?"

"Mr Fordbridge."

"Yes, him. Come on, let's go and find the fellow. I'm sure I recall seeing him drinking tea in the drawing room."

Fortunately, Mr Fordbridge was still drinking tea in the drawing room when they entered, and Churchill made a beeline for the man as soon as she spotted him. Her approach was so purposeful that he raised his teacup in a defensive manner.

"What do you want from me?" he asked warily.

"At ease, Mr Fordbridge. I just wanted to have a little chat with you."

"About what?"

"Do you recall me sitting next to you while Mr Hurricks was in this very room reciting *A Christmas Carol*?"

"No, I'm afraid I don't."

"You don't? We were sitting on that sofa just there, where that lady in the frilly blue dress is sitting now."

"I remember sitting there, yes."

"Good. Now, I wasn't present for the first ghost, but I was most definitely there for the second and part of the third," said Churchill. "He had to stop during the third one, didn't he? On account of the murder."

"I remember he had to stop, yes."

"Good. Now, do you remember me squeezing myself onto the end of the sofa during the second ghost?"

"Oh, was that you? I remember someone sitting there, yes."

"Rather snug, wasn't it? I recall you applauding at regular intervals."

"I like to do that. He's quite the storyteller, isn't he?"

"Quite! So you do remember me sitting next to you?"

"I don't recall the person specifically being you, Mrs Churchill. We were so close-quartered it would have been odd – rude, even – to turn and look at you directly."

"I know what you mean, Mr Fordbridge. It would have been a breach of etiquette. But are you satisfied now that I was seated beside you for the duration of about twenty minutes? Actually, it was probably more like fifteen minutes, because I went to the music room first and then came in here. I was instructed to come here, in fact. I was *told* I *had* to listen to Mr Hurricks!"

"Good."

Mr Fordbridge sipped his tea and Churchill wondered whether she had managed to drive home her point.

"So when Inspector Mappin asks you who was sitting next to you at the time of the murder you'll tell him, won't you?"

"Dick!"

"Dick?"

"Dick Sparrow. He was on my left."

"And on your right?"

"Was you, Mrs Churchill."

"Thank you, Mr Fordbridge."

"Or so you tell me."

"But you're quite sure of it now, aren't you?"

"I think so, but if Inspector Mappin had asked me ten minutes ago who had been sitting on my right I'd only have been able to tell him that it was a member of the fairer sex."

"Only that?"

"Well, erm… I'm not sure how to put this without causing offence. A *larger* member of the fairer sex."

"A reasonable description, Mr Fordbridge, and one that would rule out a number of the ladies gathered here. Would you have been able to include anything else in your description? Did you notice the Harris tweed skirt, for instance?"

"Tweed skirt… Yes, I think I probably noticed that."

"Good. Well then, we have our stories straight now. So at the very least you saw on your right a large member of the fairer sex wearing a tweed skirt. That describes me pretty well, doesn't it?"

He gave a nod.

"And on reflection you realised that this large lady in the tweed skirt was, in fact, Mrs Churchill."

"Yes. Can I go now?"

"No need for you to go anywhere, Mr Fordbridge. Leave the going somewhere to me."

Churchill left the drawing room with Pemberley at her heels.

"Goodness, Pembers, that was rather tiresome," she said once they were back in the corridor and out of earshot. "But quite essential, I should think. Hopefully my alibi will be watertight after all that. Now then, what about Hurricks?"

"He couldn't be the murderer. He's been far too busy boring everyone with overacted Dickens stories all evening."

"He's not a suspect, I quite agree, but I wonder whether he might be able to shed some light on the bitter feud between his mother and Mr Donkin. Rather an interesting one, isn't it?"

∼

They found Mr Hurricks in the music room enacting an improvised version of *'Twas the Night Before Christmas* alongside Father Christmas for the benefit of the children.

"He's not doing a bad job, is he?" whispered Churchill as she observed their happy faces. "Hopefully they've forgotten any mention of that unpleasant business earlier."

"Happy Christmas to all," boomed Mr Hurricks, "and to all a good night!"

He and Father Christmas took a deep bow. Miss Pauling led the applause, but although she was smiling she looked a little wan.

"That orphanage lady appears to have had her fill of Christmas entertainment," whispered Pemberley.

"She looks like she needs a stiff sherry."

"Did I hear the words '*stiff sherry*'?" asked a perspiring, red-faced Mr Hurricks as he made his way toward the door.

"You did indeed, Mr Hurricks. Though I wondered if we might have a little word with you first."

"But I've just finished a performance! I'm completely spent!"

"It won't take a moment. Would it help if the little word happened to be accompanied by a stiff sherry?"

"It'll have to be, I'm afraid. I need to refuel."

The two ladies followed his large form out of the music room toward the dining room, where decanters of sherry and little bottles of bitters were neatly arranged on the dining table. Mrs Thonnings and the old lady in the Christmas hat were already there topping up their glasses.

Mr Hurricks gave a great sigh of exhaustion as he slopped a generous measure of sherry into a glass and guzzled it down in one go. Pemberley gave Churchill a concerned glance.

"There!" he exclaimed, pouring himself another. "That's beginning to hit the spot!"

"Don't you want to add any bitters?" asked Churchill as he poured the second glass down his throat.

"Nope." He smacked his lips together. "That's really doing the job now. They make for a tough audience, children."

"I can imagine."

"They never laugh or applaud out of politeness."

"Do they not?"

"No! They demand proper entertainment. And if they don't like it, they tell you."

"Do they? Goodness!"

"There's no pulling the wool over their eyes."

"Well no, and I should hope not, either. Could you—?"

"They really tell it how it is. You've got to be made of strong stuff to perform to children."

"Yes indeed. Though I think that being made of strong stuff is rather useful for life in general. Could you—?"

"Not necessarily."

"No?"

"No. Some audiences are much kinder than that."

"Are they? That's good, then. Could you—?"

"But it can be very tough all the same."

"Yes, of course. Now, Mr Hurricks! Could you please answer a question or two for us?"

"I do apologise, I've just finished performing. This is what I'm like after a performance. Jittery!" He poured himself another sherry. "It takes me a while, it does. Takes me a while to adjust myself to not performing. It just takes me a while, that's all." He drank his third sherry, albeit at a slightly slower pace this time.

"Mr Hurricks," Churchill began.

"Yes, what is it?"

"I'd like to speak to you about your mother."

"Oh, gosh." His face softened and his shoulders slumped. "Where would you like me to start?"

"With the garden wall, actually, and the dispute she had with Mr Donkin."

He stiffened up again. "Oh, that!"

"How did the feud begin?"

"It was a long time ago now. Bob Donkin returned from the war and decided that the wall belonged to him."

"But it doesn't?"

"No. My mother looked after that wall while the Donkin brothers were away fighting, and then they suddenly returned. Well, just Bob actually. And then he wanted it back!"

"So he had owned it at one time?"

"Yes, it had belonged to the Donkin family before the war."

"So it was rightfully theirs?"

"Not at all! My mother paid for it to be repointed while they were away fighting. If she hadn't looked after that wall there would have been no wall to return to!"

"The wall feud has been going on for some time, I believe."

"Yes, about fourteen years."

"Has your mother ever expressed any wish to have Mr Donkin, erm − how shall I put this? − moved or got rid of in some way?"

"Oh yes, all the time! Every day she expresses her wish that something unfortunate should befall him. Only yesterday she said to me, 'I may be bedridden these days, son, but I'm determined to outlive that dastardly Bob Donkin and have my wall back once and for all!'"

"Good grief! Strong words indeed."

"She's made of strong stuff."

"It's safe to say, then, Mr Hurricks, that your mother may even be pleasantly surprised when she hears the news of Mr Donkin's demise."

"Without a doubt! She's sick and tired of all his comings and goings."

"What sort of comings and goings?"

"There was a lady friend visiting him just last week."

"Oh really? Who might that have been?"

"I don't know, but I heard a feminine voice through the wall."

"How very interesting."

"Not really. When he had the choir over to practise it was dreadful, though."

"The choir practised in his home?"

"Once, when the church was flooded. I was forced to

listen to the same verse of '*All Things Bright and Beautiful*' twenty-four times."

"Oh dear. You weren't tempted to go and do something else?"

"Why should I? I have every right to sit in my mother's home without being subjected to such tosh!"

"I think it's quite a nice song," commented Pemberley.

"Oh, I used to think that myself! Oh yes, I did. I used to very much think that, in fact. I used to adore that song, but he ruined it! Ruined it, I tell you!"

"Oh dear," said Churchill patiently.

Mr Hurricks drained the last of his sherry. "I'd better go outside and cool my head off in the snow."

Mrs Thonnings and the old lady in the Christmas hat watched anxiously as Mr Hurricks left the room. Once he was out of sight, they approached Churchill and Pemberley.

"You didn't ask him about his mother and the wall, did you?" asked Mrs Thonnings.

"I did," replied Churchill.

"Oh, heavens! We should have warned you never to do that!"

Chapter Nineteen

"Aha!" exclaimed Inspector Mappin as he stepped into the dining room. "There you are, Mrs Churchill!"

"Here I am indeed."

The inspector leafed through his notebook and cleared his throat.

"May I ask why you didn't include Miss Pemberley in your, er, *greeting*, if you could call it such?" asked Churchill. "'*There you are, Mrs Churchill*' isn't the politest of welcomes, and why wasn't Miss Pemberley mentioned? She is, after all, my trusty assistant. My Woman Friday, if you like."

"So she is. But Miss Pemberley isn't the one who is desperately trying to establish an alibi, is she?"

"Is she not?"

"You know she isn't. You, on the other hand, have intimidated a gentleman into stating that he was with you at the time of the murder."

"But he was! I sat next to him while we were listening to Mr Hurricks."

"I assume Mr Hurricks will also be able to vouch for that, will he?"

"Probably, though he's outside cooling his head at present."

"Why did he need to cool his head?"

"He's just finished performing."

"I see. Nothing to do with anything you might have said to him, then?"

"No."

"You do realise it's an offence to fabricate an alibi, don't you?"

"I didn't fabricate him. He's perfectly real!"

"To provide a false alibi, then. You could be getting the man into serious trouble, Mrs Churchill."

"It's not false, either. I was sitting right next to him!"

"So you say. But if this man is a proper alibi, why did you feel the need to intimidate him?"

"I didn't intimidate him, Inspector. I merely asked whether he remembered me sitting there."

"To what end?"

"I wanted to be certain that my alibi knew who I was."

"And did he?"

"He recalled that I was a large lady in a tweed skirt."

"I see. I'm sure you must realise how suspicious this all looks, Mrs Churchill. You and Miss Pemberley were the last people to see Mr Donkin alive, and at that time you were engaged in an altercation with him, which suggests a possible motive. You were in the music room at around the time the murder weapon was removed from the mantelpiece, and you were 'examining' the murder scene in the parlour when I arrived. Or perhaps you were removing evidence. In addition to all that, you were later discovered in the morning room wielding a candlestick; another possible murder weapon."

"Wielding?"

"This whole attempt to establish an alibi sounds like an

act of desperation to me. An act of desperation from a murderess who knows full well that the net is closing in on her!"

"Nonsense!" exploded Churchill. "This is all utter piffle, and you know it!"

"Right then." Inspector Mappin tucked his notebook into his pocket and folded his arms. "If you're half the sleuth you claim to be, Mrs Churchill, why don't you tell me who the real culprit is? Surely you have the detective skills to not only dig yourself out of this one but also to provide an alternative theory."

"I'm working on it, Inspector."

He gave a hollow laugh. "I imagine you are, Mrs Churchill." He unfolded his arms and walked over to the dining table, where he proceeded to pour himself a glass of sherry. "Would you like one, Mrs Churchill?"

Confused by the change in tone, she gave a slow nod.

"Miss Pemberley? Sherry?"

"Thank you. Why are you being nice to us all of a sudden, Inspector?" Pemberley asked.

"Oh, there's only so much confrontation one can put up with over the course of an evening, don't you think?" he said, handing the two ladies their sherries. "There's no need to be so adversarial about everything all the time. After all, it's nearly Christmas."

"So it is, Inspector," said Churchill, raising her glass. "Down the hatch!"

The inspector stood with one hand wrapped around his glass and the other in his pocket as he surveyed the room.

"It's rather a lovely old building, isn't it?"

"Yes, it is," replied Churchill. "I made the same remark myself not long ago."

"It's probably early nineteenth century, wouldn't you say?"

"Yes, I would most certainly say that. A very nice old place."

"I do love an old building. I remarked to the vicar earlier how marvellous these old buildings are with their countless rooms and attics and secret passageways."

"Secret passageways?"

"Yes. Do you suppose the vicarage has one?"

Churchill stared back at him, stumped for words.

"Perhaps you already knew that the vicarage had a secret passageway," suggested the inspector, holding her gaze. "Perhaps you've even seen it."

Churchill considered several scenarios in her mind all at once. If she denied knowing about the secret passageway Inspector Mappin would surely catch her in a lie, but if she admitted it she might further convince him of her involvement in the murder.

She glanced at Pemberley, who stared blankly back at her, her face offering no useful answers at all.

"Er... secret passageway, you say, Inspector?" she stammered.

"Yes. Have you come across one in the vicarage?"

"Erm... As a matter of fact we have, yes." Churchill hoped she had done the right thing in admitting it.

"Interesting," replied the inspector with a nod. "Very interesting indeed."

He finished his sherry and placed his glass on the dining table.

"Mrs Churchill, I need to take a precaution, and I hope that in doing so it won't cause too much inconvenience to yourself. I need to ask you and Miss Pemberley to adjourn to the vicar's study, and I must ask your permission to lock you up in there for a while."

"Lock us in the vicar's study? Good grief, Inspector! Whatever for?"

"I need to gather a few more pieces of information, but that won't take me long at all, so I can confidently say to you now that it won't be for any longer than an hour."

"But why lock us anywhere, Inspector?"

"It's just a precaution. I don't want you taking off anywhere, nor do I want you conversing with anyone else at this party. If it helps, I understand that the cook, Mrs Robertson, has baked a fresh batch of mince pies, which will be made available in the study for you to enjoy at your leisure. I promise it'll be no more than an hour."

"And if we refuse?"

"Then I might just have to arrest you for obstruction of justice."

"Great goodness! To state that I'm shocked would be a vast understatement, Inspector. Do you plan to arrest us after we've been locked in the study for an hour?"

"That all depends on this last line of inquiry I intend to follow up on."

Chapter Twenty

"I never should have admitted that we knew about the secret passageway, should I?" Churchill said glumly as she sat at the vicar's writing desk in his study. "Now Mappin's certain we're the murderers, and he supposedly only has one last inquiry to make. What could that possibly be?"

"Oh, I don't know!" whimpered Pemberley as she paced the floor. "I can't believe he's locked us away in the vicar's study. It's barbaric! I hate being shut up in places. If it's for any longer than an hour I shall climb out of the window!"

"That's not a bad idea, Pembers. I shan't be following you, though. I haven't been particularly proficient at escaping through windows since I began my career as a private detective. Oh, darn it! I wish I knew which last inquiry Mappin was referring to. Unless he's just calling our bluff in the hope that we'll cave and confess."

"Oh, it's completely hopeless. Hopeless! I wish we'd never come to the Vicarage Christmas Party!"

"So do I, Pembers. We could have just left them to get

on with this whole murder business by themselves. They'd have been stuck then, wouldn't they?"

"They wouldn't even have suspected us, instead they'd have had to look for the real murderer!"

"Exactly. Who do you think it might be? I was so sure we had our man with Mr Swipplekirk, but then I had my doubts when Mrs Stonecastle told us about the passageway."

"I think most people know about the passageway, so having prior knowledge of it doesn't necessarily tell us anything."

"Old Hurricks has a strong motive, but there can be no doubt that he was reciting *A Christmas Carol* at the time. Perhaps he convinced someone to carry out the murder on his behalf."

"He could have done, but which someone might that have been?"

"Good question. There's still a possibility that it was the vicar, don't you think?"

"I do indeed, especially now that he seems so convinced of our guilt. He openly accused you of being a murderer, didn't he? All because you were caught placing that candlestick back on the mantelpiece!"

"Very quick to level that accusation at me, wasn't he? It's the sort of thing a man with a guilty conscience might do."

"But I still can't believe that a man of the cloth would commit murder."

"I suppose anyone can be a suspect, which explains how two old ladies have come to be locked in the study. Still, I suppose there are worse prisons," said Churchill. "There's a plate of mince pies here, at least. In fact, it feels rather nice to be sitting down for an hour. I'm quite fatigued, if truth be told. We've had non-stop capers ever since we arrived at this dreadful party. This hour will give us an opportunity to mull over the case and indulge in a mince pie or two as we do so. The hour will soon pass, I'm sure."

"And after that we'll be arrested!"

"In which case we have an hour to find the culprit." Churchill took a bite of warm mince pie.

"But how can we when we're locked in the study? It's impossible, Mrs Churchill!"

"Come and sit down with a nice mince pie, Pembers."

"A mince pie can't save us now!"

"Maybe not, but it's better than pacing the floor like that. You'll wear a hole in the vicar's nice rug if you carry on. Now then, there are plenty of books in here. Perhaps there are some interesting ones we can browse and while away the time."

"I'm not in the mood for reading now. But perhaps one of the bookcases leads to another secret passageway."

"Of course! What an ingenious thought!" Churchill gulped down the last bite of her mince pie and leapt up out of her seat. "Let's try this one!" She stepped over to the nearest bookcase and began tugging at one side of it. "Can you help me shift it, Pembers?"

The two ladies pushed and pulled with all their might, but to no avail. Then they tried another bookcase leaning against the opposite wall, but that one also failed to move.

Churchill flopped back into her chair with a sigh. "I suppose it was wishful thinking. And if the inspector knows all about the secret passageways in this vicarage, he was hardly likely to lock us in a room with one, was he?"

Pemberley sank into a chair beside the fire. "It explains why the morning room was locked earlier, though. Inspector Mappin must have known about the entrance to the secret passageway and didn't want anyone making their escape that way."

"Pah! He's marginally cleverer than we thought, isn't he? He's still a great lumbering beefhead, though."

The two ladies sat in thoughtful silence as they steadily worked their way through the plate of mince pies. Churchill quietly hoped that her trusty assistant would be struck with a sudden flash of inspiration, but as she watched Pemberley sadly nibbling at a mince pie, her tired cardigan hanging off her slumped shoulders, her heart sank. She closed her eyes for a moment and waited for a flash of inspiration to strike her instead. She felt sure that something someone had told her that evening had to be pertinent. But what?

She opened her eyes again to see Pemberley still looking slumped and glum.

The clock on the wall showed that there were forty minutes left before Inspector Mappin was due to fetch them.

Did he really intend to arrest them? Was there truly enough evidence to suggest that they'd been involved in Mr Donkin's murder? If so, perhaps they were being framed.

Churchill gave a shudder. She knew they had to do something to fix the situation. She helped herself to a sheet of the vicar's letter paper and dipped a pen into his ink pot.

"Right then, let's write everything down. I'm sure it'll make more sense once it's all written down."

She spent the next few minutes scribbling down people's names and the snippets of information they had given her. Then she linked relevant words together with lines and arrows.

"It's almost like a miniature incident board, Pembers. What do you think?"

The two ladies stared at it for a while, but nothing new sprang to mind.

"Oh, I don't know, Pembers. How about we rummage through the vicar's personal effects instead?"

"I don't think he'd like us to do that."

"Of course he wouldn't, but seeing as we've been locked in his study I think we've earned ourselves the right to do so."

Churchill tried opening a few of the drawers in the vicar's writing desk. "Oh dear, these ones are locked."

Pemberley sighed. "I knew it."

"There must be other personal effects somewhere that we can riffle through."

Churchill rose to her feet and started scrutinising shelves and opening cabinets.

"I've found his drinks cabinet, Pembers. We can make good use of that if all else fails."

Pemberley joined her. "What exactly are we looking for?"

"I don't really know. Anything intriguing among the vicar's personal effects, I suppose."

"I'm not sure how that will help us."

"Me neither at this stage, but we may as well make some use of our time here. Let's suppose for a moment that the vicar is trying to frame us."

"He wouldn't do something like that, would he?"

"I don't know, but it's a possibility. Perhaps he and Mappin are in on it together. If we could find something damning against the vicar, it could be used as a bargaining tool."

"I can't imagine the vicar leaving anything damning lying around."

"Me neither, but it's worth a look. After all, there's nothing else to do now that we've eaten all the mince pies."

Pemberley opened a cabinet beside the fireplace. "Here are some old photo albums."

"Are there any embarrassing pictures of the vicar we can use as a bargaining tool?"

"I'll have a look."

"I was joking, Pembers. We need something more than an embarrassing photograph to help our cause." Churchill stood with her hands on her hips and looked around the room. "There has to be something useful here!"

Her thoughts were interrupted by a loud burst of laughter from Pemberley.

"Good grief, Pembers! What's so funny?"

"Mrs Thonnings's hat!"

Churchill strode over to where Pemberley was leafing through the photograph albums. "Feathers in hats were all the rage back then, weren't they? But surely not feathers as big as that!" Pemberley pointed to a photograph that showed a group of women having a picnic beside a river.

"Is that really Mrs Thonnings?"

"Yes! It must have been taken about twenty years ago."

"She was quite a beauty back then, wasn't she?"

"I suppose she was. There she is again with Mr Bodkin the baker."

"Oh yes. What's he holding in his hand?"

"A slingshot, I think. Oh my, I remember that tea party at the vicarage. I was just visiting for a few weeks, because in those days I was still employed as a companion—"

"To a lady of international travel."

"Yes. Oh gosh, there's Mr Atkins! Oh!" Pemberley clapped her hand over her mouth as if she were trying to quell the emotion of suddenly being faced with a photograph of her deceased former employer.

"That's what he looked like, is it?" Churchill peered

down at the slight, dark-haired man with the dark mous-tache. "Is that Mappin he's standing next to?"

"Yes."

"Goodness, I had no idea Mappin was in possession of all that hair back then!"

"He was indeed. The girls were all very fond of it in his youth."

Churchill gave a snort. "I wouldn't have been."

"Here's the vicar."

"Oh good. Is it an embarrassing photograph we can bribe him with?"

"I'm afraid not. He's just posing beside the first motor car we had in the village at the time. I believe it was owned by Mr Crumble."

"The proprietor of the Piddleton Hotel? Pah! Dreadful man."

"And here's Colonel Slingsby with a large carp."

Churchill sighed. "Most of these photographs are rather dull."

"Quite funny, though, when you know the people in them. Oh, goodness! There's Mr Donkin and his brother."

"Where?"

"Here." Pemberley pointed to a photograph of two men standing next to a postbox. "It was the day the new postbox outside the town hall was officially opened."

"Quite alike, weren't they?"

"Yes, but you could tell them apart by the birthmark on Hector's neck. And Bob had a wonderful singing voice, whereas Hector couldn't sing for toffee. Sad to think that they're both deceased now. And there's Mrs Furzgate," continued Pemberley, "another one who is now deceased. And Tubby Williams as well. Oh dear…"

The two ladies were interrupted by the sound of a key turning in the lock.

"Mappin!" exclaimed Churchill, "and he's fifteen minutes early!"

"Oh no, we're for it now!" said Pemberley. "He's finished making his last line of inquiry and we're about to be arrested!"

Chapter Twenty-One

"Good evening, ladies," said Inspector Mappin as he swung open the study door. "You'll be pleased to know that I completed my investigation sooner than expected, so there's no need to detain you in the study for a moment longer."

"Why, thank you, Inspector," replied Churchill. "The entire incident was uncalled for if you ask me, but I suppose that's the way you like to do things."

"Come along with me, please. We'd better go and meet with the vicar in the morning room."

"May I ask why, Inspector?" Churchill asked as they left the study and moved into the corridor.

"Yes, I may as well explain it to you now, Mrs Churchill. The fact of the matter is that you don't have an alibi for the time that Mr Donkin was murdered."

"No alibi? All my eye and Betty Martin!" scorned Churchill. "I was sitting next to that tartan-jacketed Fordbridge fellow. What's wrong with the man?"

"After extensive questioning, we have determined that he cannot be certain that it was you who was sitting next to him during the performance. We have identified another lady at the party who is of a... aherm... a larger size, and also wears a tweed skirt."

"Who might that be? She sounds like my sort of woman."

"Mrs Briscote."

"Never heard of her."

"So it could have been you sitting next to Mr Fordbridge or it could have been Mrs Briscote."

"How ridiculous, Inspector! Surely there are other witnesses. I was in a room full of people!"

"I've asked Mr Hurricks, but he says he was too absorbed in his performance to identify whether specific members of the audience were present or not."

"Is that so? Then I wish I'd never bothered sitting through that infernal recital! Is that his voice I hear now?"

Stentorian tones boomed from the drawing room once again as they approached it.

"Yes," replied the inspector. "He's performing a rendition of the nativity now."

"By himself?"

"Yes. I've seen him do it before, in fact. He's good at doing all the different voices, you know. He has quite a range. The vicar asked him to put on another performance to keep everyone entertained. They're getting quite restless, having been detained in the vicarage all evening."

"I know the feeling."

"Anyway, it won't be for much longer. I just have a few procedural matters to go through and then everyone will be free to go."

Churchill paused outside the door to the drawing room. "Will Miss Pemberley and I be free to go, Inspector?"

Inspector Mappin paused as his mouth tried to form a

reply. Churchill sensed that the answer would have been no had Mr Hurricks not provided a distraction at that moment.

"No room at the inn!" he boomed to his audience, jutting his jaw out authoritatively.

Churchill glanced into the drawing room and saw that it was filled with all the party attendees.

Here was her opportunity to publicly plead her innocence. Or was it possible that she had a theory of her own to propose?

Without further ado, Churchill stepped into the drawing room. "Come on, Pembers," she muttered. "In here!"

"Mrs Churchill," Inspector Mappin said reproachfully. "You're supposed to be coming with me!"

The two ladies edged their way through the audience toward Mr Hurricks, who was standing beside the Christmas tree at the far end of the drawing room.

"Mrs Churchill!" the inspector called out.

Heads turned.

"I beg your pardon!" cried Mr Hurricks, who was busy taking the part of the innkeeper's wife showing Joseph and Mary into the stable. "I'm in the middle of a performance, Inspector!"

"Just a brief interlude, Mr Hurricks," chimed Churchill as she reached him. "Inspector Mappin's just off to fetch the vicar, aren't you, Inspector?"

He glared at her from the doorway.

"Well, go on then, Inspector," she added. "Everyone's waiting!"

"May I ask the reason for this impertinence?" boomed Mr Hurricks.

"Yes, you may. A poor gentleman lost his life here at the Vicarage Christmas Party this evening, and while I realise you're mid-performance, Mr Hurricks, I rather think we need to get to the bottom of what happened so the culprit can be held to account for his actions."

"I had nothing to do with it, if that's what you're insinuating!"

"I hope that all will become clear shortly, Mr Hurricks, and then you can resume your performance. Or perhaps everyone would prefer to return home."

"Hear, hear!" Mrs Stonecastle called out.

"I want to go home!" exclaimed the lady in the Christmas hat. "I've had enough!"

Mr Hurricks scowled.

"Mrs Churchill," whispered Pemberley. "Would you mind telling me what's going on before the vicar gets here?"

"Of course, my adjutant. Here's my theory, and I shall be interested to hear what you make of it."

Chapter Twenty-Two

CHURCHILL HAD JUST enough time to whisper her theory into Pemberley's ear before the vicar arrived with the inspector in tow.

"Mrs Churchill!" called the vicar from the doorway. "Will you please join me and the inspector in the morning room?"

"I certainly will in just a moment, Vicar," she replied.

"Please do so now and allow Mr Hurricks to continue entertaining the guests."

"I shall just have a quick word with your guests about my theory as to who the murderer is, and then I shall join you right away, Vicar. I would highly recommend that you and the inspector stay and listen in the meantime."

"There's no need for all this, Mrs Churchill," retorted the vicar. "The inspector has already completed his work on the case, and we've asked you politely to join us without delay."

"We want to hear what she has to say!" called out the lady in the frilly blue dress.

"I just want to hear a voice that isn't Hurricks's," added the man with the large nose.

"Mrs Churchill," warned the inspector. "Come here immediately!"

"The guests assembled here would like me to tell them my theory about the murder of Mr Donkin, Inspector. I shall be as brief as I can, and then everything can continue as normal."

"And I can go home," added the old lady in the Christmas hat.

"Just let Mrs Churchill say her piece, Inspector," said Mrs Thonnings. "I like it when she gets to this bit!"

"Fine!" barked the inspector, clearly sensing that he had few people on his side. "You have three minutes, Mrs Churchill."

"As long as that?" moaned Mr Hurricks.

"Thank you, everyone," said Churchill, "I shall speak as succinctly as possible. Now, it goes without saying that this Christmas party has been a rather odd and difficult one. We lost a guest who himself stood in this very spot just a few hours ago, conducting the Compton Poppleford Choir through a medley of delightful and jolly Christmas songs. That was the highlight of the Christmas party for me, and it's terribly sad that the evening should suddenly have turned so sour when, a short while after that perfor-mance, Mr Donkin was savagely stabbed in the back with the vicar's ornamental letter opener.

"But who did it? That's the question on everyone's lips this evening. And *why* did the murderer do it? That's another question, and it's one that my trusty assistant Miss Pemberley and I have been deliberating over ever since poor Bob Donkin was found dead in the parlour by Mrs Stonecastle at ten minutes to seven this evening."

Sympathetic faces turned toward Mrs Stonecastle, who gave a sad nod.

"Perhaps the culprit was a member of the choir," said Churchill. "So angered were they all at being lambasted by the choirmaster – which I felt was entirely unwarranted given the excellent standard of their performance – that a member of the choir was driven to murder as an act of revenge."

"It wasn't me!" Mr Swipplekirk called out.

"One point that is most interesting," continued Churchill, fixing Mr Swipplekirk with both eyes, "is that no one appeared to see the murderer on his way to or from the parlour this evening. There's a possibility that the murderer made use of the secret passageway that runs between the morning room and the parlour. The entrances to the passageway are sealed behind two bookcases, potentially allowing the murderer to slip into and away from the parlour unseen."

"Good grief! Is that right?" asked Mr Hurricks.

"It is. So might our murderer have been someone who knew about this secret passageway?"

"He must have been!" replied Mr Hurricks.

"You knew about the secret passageway, didn't you, Mr Swipplekirk?" Churchill asked, her eyes still fixed on him.

Mr Swipplekirk shifted in his seat. "I, er... I've heard about it, but I can't say that I know a great deal other than that it exists."

"You certainly knew about it when I spoke to you earlier, Mr Swipplekirk."

"Did I? Perhaps I did, yes."

"And you were rather angry with Mr Donkin when he shouted at you."

Mr Swipplekirk's face reddened. "That's hardly

surprising, is it? We all were! I didn't murder him if that's what you're suggesting, Mrs Churchill!"

A number of faces had turned toward Mr Swipplekirk.

"I didn't do it!" he said beseechingly. "If someone were to bring me one of the vicar's Bibles this very moment and ask me to swear my innocence upon it I would happily do so!"

"There's no need to go to such lengths at the present moment, Mr Swipplekirk," continued Churchill. "I should add that another person who knew about the passageway was your fellow choir member, Mrs Stonecastle."

Mrs Stonecastle gave a gasp. "But I... Oh!"

The old lady in the Christmas hat gently patted her shoulder. "She's not a murderer, Mrs Churchill. I was the one who told her about the secret passageway. Does that make me a murderer, too?"

"Not necessarily, Mrs..."

"Besides, she's the one who discovered him," continued the old lady. "How could she have gone down the passageway, murdered him, come back up the passageway and then gone round the normal way and found him? And why would she have gone to find him if she's the murderer? Wouldn't she have let someone else do that?"

"All very good points, Mrs..."

"And she wouldn't have had any reason to do it, anyway. She's only been living here a month!"

"All right. Thank you, Mrs... Let me move on with the rest of my theory. Mr Hurricks, I believe you detested Mr Donkin, am I right?"

He responded with a glower. "You already know that, and we don't really need to dredge it all up again, Mrs Churchill."

"Your good mother had no time for him either, did she?"

"She didn't, no. But I must warn you that you're going to make me very cross bringing this subject up again, Mrs Churchill!"

"But you couldn't have possibly murdered Mr Donkin because you were in this room the whole time performing *A Christmas Carol*."

"I was indeed, and I never reached the end of it!"

"That's because some poor chap lost his life just as you were approaching the finale. When a murder occurs, it tends to take precedence over other matters of the day. Now, I do wonder, Mr Hurricks, whether there's a possibility that you became so enraged about the altercation between your dear mother and Mr Donkin that you arranged for someone else to do away with him."

"You think I hired someone to kill Donkin?" he fumed. "Utter balderdash! And even if I had, do you think I would have arranged the timing of it to coincide with one of my performances?"

"No, I must concede that doing so would have been most unlikely," replied Churchill. "However, you did mention that a lady friend visited Mr Donkin last week."

"Yes, that's right. Just one of his usual comings and goings. I don't see what that's got to do with anything."

"That's something I'll come back to in a short while, Mr Hurricks."

"Have you finished, Mrs Churchill?" Inspector Mappin piped up. "I think it's been almost three minutes."

"Nearly there, Inspector. Now then, this secret passageway…"

"It's quite simple," interrupted the vicar. "We'll ask everyone who knew about the secret passageway to stand on one side of the room and everyone who didn't to stand on the other. That should separate out the potential murderers from the innocents."

"And let's not forget that you knew about the secret passageway yourself, Mrs Churchill," added Inspector Mappin.

"Only in the aftermath of Mr Donkin's tragic demise, Inspector. Miss Pemberley and I discovered it by pure chance."

"You can't prove that."

"No one can prove one way or the other whether they knew about the passageway that leads from the morning room to the parlour. And it's quite irrelevant anyhow, Inspector, because the murderer didn't use it."

Inspector Mappin gave a snort of derision. "Then how on earth did the murderer enter and leave the scene of the crime without anyone noticing him?"

"Oh, but people did notice the murderer," replied Churchill. "Because the murderer was making quite a song and dance when the crime occurred."

"What?" scoffed the vicar. "I certainly didn't hear him! Did anyone else hear him?"

There was a general shaking of heads in response.

"*Her*," Churchill corrected him. "The murderer is a lady."

"What?!" said the vicar incredulously.

"Mrs Stonecastle," stated Churchill calmly.

She stared at the woman, who bowed her curly-haired head.

"But it can't be," the old lady in the Christmas hat cried out. "She's been here less than a month!"

"Exactly," replied Churchill. "And therein lies the clue."

"How ridiculous!" the vicar called out.

"Mrs Churchill," said Inspector Mappin, pushing his way through the guests as he made his way toward her, "I realise you've managed to solve a few crimes since you arrived in this village, but I'm beginning to think that you've concocted this rather embarrassing display to distract me from the main thrust of my investigation. Please come with me now and we'll clear this matter up somewhere a little more private."

Churchill glared at him. "I haven't finished, Inspector."

"Mrs Stonecastle has been extremely upset by this evening's events," he fumed. "And to be labelled a murderess is sheer cruelty. I fear you'd do anything at this point to shift the blame from yourself."

"Hear her out!" cried Pemberley, startling Inspector Mappin with her uncharacteristic outburst.

"I agree," Mr Hurricks chipped in. "Let's hear why Mrs Churchill has chosen to accuse poor Mrs Stonecastle of murder. I'm quite enjoying this performance, I must say. It's almost as entertaining as something I might have put on!"

Inspector Mappin scowled at Churchill. "You have one minute to explain why you think Mrs Stonecastle carried out the murder."

"One minute? Really, Inspector? Why do you always insist on putting time limits on things?"

"Mrs Stonecastle would never do such a thing!" Mrs Thonnings called out.

"Why Mrs Stonecastle?" yelled the man with the large nose.

Churchill glanced over at the lady in question and saw that she was covering her face with her hands.

She cleared her throat. "Right, then. Here goes."

Chapter Twenty-Three

"IT's QUITE SIMPLE, REALLY," said Churchill as everyone stared at her in silence. "When Mrs Stonecastle claimed to have discovered the murder, she had actually just committed it herself."

Gasps resounded around the room.

"The distress she displayed when she ran out of the parlour was little more than a clever act," continued Churchill. "After all, who would believe that this innocent-looking lady, who had just won the coveted Christmas cake competition, could have plunged the vicar's ornamental letter opener into the choirmaster's back?"

"But why would she?" said Mr Hurricks. "We're still none the wiser!"

"Mr Donkin was quite cross with us," called out Mr Swipplekirk, "but none of us felt that he deserved to be stabbed in the back."

"I doubt the motive was prompted only by Mr Donkin's outburst of temper this evening," replied Churchill. "Let me remind you all of an event that occurred here eighteen years ago. Bob Donkin and his brother Hector journeyed to Paris, where Bob Donkin met—"

"Oh no, not that ridiculous village gossip again," interrupted Inspector Mappin. "That's just a story Bob Donkin came up with to explain why he never married."

"Quiet!" called out the lady in the frilly blue dress. "I want to hear what she has to say!"

"Thank you, Mrs… Anyway, where was I?" said Churchill. "Oh yes. Some of you will be familiar with this tale, so I shall present it as succinctly as possible and take questions afterwards. Bob Donkin fell in love with a Prussian princess, only to discover that she was engaged to be married to a princeling of some sort. He returned to Compton Poppleford broken-hearted and certain that he would never see her again. The princess escaped to this very village a short while later and called at Bob Donkin's home, only to encounter his brother Hector Donkin. Hector told her to meet Bob at the packhorse bridge but failed to tell Bob that she was there waiting for him. Sadly, the two lovers were never reunited. The brothers subsequently went away to war, where Hector Donkin lost his life.

"Bob Donkin returned to Compton Poppleford, changed by his wartime experiences. No one ever knew what became of the princess; we can only guess that she was eventually married to her princeling. Years later her circumstances changed… Perhaps the princess became widowed. We don't know exactly what caused her to return, but, remembering her true love she returned to Compton Poppleford to find him again."

"So they were reunited," the old lady in the Christmas hat called out happily, "but then he got murdered!"

"Not quite," replied Churchill. "The princess, perhaps I can use her proper name now – Princess Wilhelmina

Herzeleide Alexandrine von der Steinburg – did meet Bob Donkin. She even joined his choir, and I suspect she was the lady visitor who Mr Donkin received at his home last week. Now, none of us can be certain about what passed between them, but I think it's fairly safe to say that there was some dissatisfaction on the princess's part."

"On what grounds?" Mrs Thonnings shouted.

"Because the man she thought was Bob Donkin wasn't her true love after all," replied Churchill. "He was Hector Donkin!"

Gasps of astonishment were followed by a mixture of excitable chatter and shouts of denial.

"Impossible!" someone called out.

"How do you know that?" called out another.

"Yes, how *do* you know that, Mrs Churchill?" asked Inspector Mappin. "It's an astonishing claim to make."

Churchill waited for the chatter to die down.

"Quiet now!" ordered Mr Hurricks.

"A short while ago, my trusty assistant Miss Pemberley and I were locked inside the vicar's study."

"Really?" asked Mr Hurricks.

"Yes, on the instructions of Inspector Mappin."

"You locked two old ladies in the study, Inspector?" said Mr Hurricks accusingly. "That's a bit off, isn't it?"

Inspector Mappin looked ready to embark on an explanation, but Churchill interrupted just in time.

"It's just as well that he did, as Miss Pemberley and I had a bit of time to look through the vicar's old photograph albums. In fact, there wasn't a great deal else to do in there. Miss Pemberley showed me a photograph of Bob and Hector Donkin together, and I confess that it piqued my interest. Not only did they bear a striking resemblance to one another, but Hector Donkin had quite a distinctive birthmark on the left side of his neck.

A port wine stain, I think it's called by some. I didn't know the Donkin brothers, but am I correct in my summation?"

Her question was greeted with nods.

"Good. Well, I wonder how many of you observed that the man we assumed to be Bob Donkin was wearing a tightly tied cravat around his neck this evening. It was quite a distinctive cravat with a festive design, in fact. Did he always wear a cravat?"

"Yes," replied Mr Hurricks, "He did."

"Since his return from the war?"

"Yes, every day," said Mrs Thonnings.

"But Bob Donkin didn't have a birthmark on his neck," said the old lady in the Christmas hat. "That was Hector Donkin."

"Exactly, Mrs… During our altercation in the parlour this evening he was quite hot under the collar and pulled at his cravat, as if to loosen it a little. When he did so, I noticed quite a distinctive birthmark on his neck. I thought very little of it at the time, of course; in fact, I only recalled it when I saw the photograph of the two brothers side by side."

"Impossible!" someone called out.

"Well, it can be easily verified, I suppose," said Inspector Mappin. "I'll telephone the chap at the mortuary in just a moment and ask him to check."

"Thank you, Inspector Mappin."

"Then it was Hector Donkin all along?" asked Mr Hurricks. "That means it was the nice one, Bob, who was killed in the war."

"Indeed, Mr Hurricks. Having made himself unpopular with most of the villagers before he went away to fight, Hector Donkin assumed the identity of his deceased brother upon his return. Perhaps he wished to start again with a clean slate, or perhaps he had hoped that one day the Prussian princess would return."

"And so she did!" the old lady in the Christmas hat cried out. "But where is she now?"

"She's sitting next to you, Mrs…"

"What?"

"Yes! The lady we have come to know as Mrs Stonecastle is, in reality, Princess Wilhelmina Herzeleide Alexandrine von der Steinburg."

Inspector Mappin laughed out loud. "How do you figure that?"

"There is actually a clue in her English name," added Churchill. "My German is a little rusty, but I believe that 'Stonecastle' is a literal translation of 'Steinburg'."

"Is that so?" exclaimed Mr Hurricks. "My, my. What a fine actress!"

The lady who had sat listening with her head slumped finally rose to her feet. Her face was red and her eyes were watery.

"Yes, it's true!" she called out. "I came back here to find Bob. My husband had died so I returned to ask Bob Donkin why he never came to meet me at the packhorse bridge. That was when he told me that his evil brother had never given him my message. I was so distraught that we had lost all those years we could have spent together, but I was deeply happy that I had finally found him again.

"Only he wasn't the same as before. I knew he had fought in the war, but that didn't explain why he was no longer the kind man I remembered in Paris. And there was something about him that reminded me of Hector, the evil brother who had tried to seduce me behind Bob's back in Paris and had never told my true love that I was waiting for him that day!"

There was a general shaking of disapproving heads.

"So I visited him at his home and I asked him. I said to him, 'Are you Hector?' and he laughed. And I asked him to show me his neck, because I remembered the *Muttermal*... What is it again? Birthmark. But he kept his scarf around his neck and wouldn't show me, and then I knew! I didn't want to kill him at this wonderful party, but when he made a small boy cry that proved too much for me. I hated the man so much! I saw the knife on the mantelpiece, and–"

"Ornamental letter opener," corrected Pemberley.

"And that's when I took it. I walked back into the parlour and I didn't really have a plan, but I was angry! I asked him again if he was Hector, and he laughed at me. Then he said that he had to get his baton fixed, so he turned his back on me. And that was when I did it! I'm so sorry I spoiled the party."

A stunned silence followed.

"Well..." began Inspector Mappin.

"It sounds as though he got what he deserved," said the old lady in the Christmas hat.

"Thank you for telling us your story, Princess von der Steinburg," said Churchill.

"Please, Mrs Stonecastle is fine."

"I'm impressed by the way you perfected your English accent and managed to fool everyone into thinking you were just an ordinary person rather than a German aristocrat!"

"I left that life behind a long time ago. I never returned to my homeland or that princeling. I went to live in Weston-Super-Mare and married a man named Walter, who died earlier this year. When I came back here I tried my best to fit in."

"And you fitted in very well indeed," said Mrs Thonnings. "You even won the Christmas cake competition!

Please don't arrest her, Inspector. I think she was quite justified in getting rid of that nasty Hector Donkin."

"I'm afraid murder is murder, Mrs Thonnings," replied the inspector. "Would you mind stepping this way, Mrs Stonecastle? I'll escort you down to the station."

Mrs Stonecastle walked over and he fastened her wrists with his handcuffs.

"Inspector?" Mrs Churchill called out.

"Yes, Mrs Churchill."

"What was your theory as to how the murder took place?"

"I was still in the process of working on it, Mrs Churchill. As things stand, I shall have plenty of paper-work to complete, so if you'll all excuse me I'll get on with it right away."

Everyone watched as Inspector Mappin escorted Mrs Stonecastle from the room.

"A Prussian princess!" exclaimed Mr Hurricks. "Who'd have thought it?"

"Mrs Churchill," the vicar said, bustling over to her. "Please accept my sincerest apologies for accusing you of such a dreadful act when you clearly had nothing to do with it."

"Thank you, Vicar. My advice would be not to listen too closely to Inspector Mappin next time."

"Hopefully there won't be a next time!"

"Hopefully not. May I ask, Vicar, how you – or anyone else for that matter – failed to notice the large birthmark on Mr Donkin's neck?"

"That's a very good question, Mrs Churchill. I suppose he always wore those cravats, didn't he? And we all assumed he was Bob because he told us he was, so no one ever had any reason to doubt it. And although I recall the birthmark now, I couldn't remember which brother had it, to be quite honest with you. They were quite alike to look at, you know. I suppose it took someone who had fallen in love with one of them to notice the difference."

"I suppose it did."

"I would be honoured if you and Miss Pemberley would come and enjoy some sherry, bitters and mince pies with me in the dining room. I really must express my apologies and gratitude a little more heartily."

"Thank you Vicar, but we'd rather be on our way."

Chapter Twenty-Four

A FEW DAYS later Churchill found herself trudging through the snowy lane in her sturdy wellington boots. A robin hopped onto a snow-filled window box and eyed her cautiously. Snow rested on the windowpanes of the crooked houses that lined the lane, and smoke curled up from the white-laced chimney pots.

A thick layer of snow covered the doorstep of the house with the pea-green door. Paw prints left next to a larger set of boot prints hinted at the identity of the occupants within.

Churchill knocked at the door and it was soon answered.

"Mrs Churchill!" said a surprised Pemberley when she opened it. "No Richmond-upon-Thames for you this Christmas?"

"The branch line to Dorchester is completely snowed in, Pembers. Fancy a game of backgammon? I've brought it with me." Churchill gestured toward the basket she was holding in her right hand. "Along with a few other sundry items, of course, such as a drop of sherry and some rather delightful tea, which a good friend posted to me while she was travelling in Ceylon."

"How I should love to be in Ceylon again," said Pemberley, wistfully gazing out at the snowy lane.

"It would be a darn sight warmer than here, that's for sure. Are you going to let me in, Pembers?"

"Oh yes! Please do come in, Mrs Churchill."

"Thank you." She stamped the snow from her wellingtons onto the doormat. "There's a rather lovely smell in here. Have you been baking?"

"I have, actually. I don't often bake, but… well, in all honesty I suspected that the branch line to Dorchester might be closed, which left me wondering whether you would seek out some alternative company."

"You were perfectly correct, Pembers."

"So I took the step of making us our very own mince pie mountain!"

"Oh, how wonderful. The best Christmas present ever!"

"It's just in the kitchen through here," said Pemberley, walking on through the little doorway.

Churchill took off her boots and followed.

"At least, it *was* in here," said Pemberley, her eyes fixed on the small kitchen table, which was littered with half-nibbled mince pies. "Oswald!"

Churchill peered under the table to find the little dog sitting there, wide-eyed, with a mince pie between his jaws.

"He's down here."

"Oh, Oswald, you naughty dog, I can't leave you alone for two minutes!" scolded Pemberley. "Just look at what you've done to Mrs Churchill's mince pie mountain!"

"Don't worry about it, Pembers, it's Christmas after all." Churchill eyed the mess on the table. "I'd say that most of them are salvageable, wouldn't you? It's not the first time I've eaten mince pies that have already been nibbled. And I suspect that it won't be the last, either."

Pemberley smiled. "I'll put the kettle on."

"Thank you, my trusty assistant." Churchill made herself comfortable at the kitchen table and helped herself to a mince pie. "And thank you for baking these. They look delicious."

"I would save your compliments until after you've eaten one if I were you, Mrs Churchill. Merry Christmas!"

"And a Merry Christmas to you too, Pemberley."

The End

~

Thank you

~

Thank you for reading *Christmas Calamity at the Vicarage*, I really hope you enjoyed it!

Would you like to know when I release new books? Here are some ways to stay updated:

- Join my mailing list and receive the short story *A Troublesome Case*: emilyorgan.com/a-troublesome-case
- Like my Facebook page: facebook.com/emilyorganwriter
- Follow me on Goodreads: goodreads.com/emily_organ
- Follow me on BookBub: bookbub.com/authors/emily-organ
- View my other books here: emilyorgan.com

And if you have a moment, I would be very grateful if you would leave a quick review of *Christmas Calamity at the Vicarage* online. Honest reviews of my books help other readers discover them too!

Get a free short mystery

~

Want more of Churchill & Pemberley? Get a copy of my free short mystery *A Troublesome Case* and sit down to enjoy a thirty minute read.

Churchill and Pemberley are on the train home from a shopping trip when they're caught up with a theft from a suitcase. Inspector Mappin accuses them of stealing the valuables, but in an unusual twist of fate the elderly sleuths are forced to come to his aid!

Visit my website to claim your FREE copy:
emilyorgan.com/a-troublesome-case
Or scan this code:

Get a free short mystery

The Churchill & Pemberley Series

Join senior sleuths Churchill and Pemberley as they tackle cake and crime in an English village.

Growing bored in the autumn of her years, Londoner Annabel Churchill buys a private detective agency in a Dorset village. The purchase brings with it the eccentric Doris Pemberley and the two ladies are soon solving mysteries and chasing down miscreants in sleepy Compton Poppleford.

Plenty of characters are out to scupper their chances, among them grumpy Inspector Mappin. Another challenge is their four-legged friend who means well but has a problem with discipline.

But the biggest challenge is one which threatens to derail every case they work on: will there be enough tea and cake?

Find out more here: emilyorgan.com/the-churchill-pemberley-cozy-mystery-series

The Penny Green Series

Also by Emily Organ. Escape to 1880s London! A page-turning historical mystery series.

As one of the first female reporters on 1880s Fleet Street, plucky Penny Green has her work cut out. Whether it's investigating the mysterious death of a friend or reporting on a serial killer in the slums, Penny must rely on her wits and determination to discover the truth.

Fortunately she can rely on the help of Inspector James Blakely of Scotland Yard, but will their relationship remain professional?

Find out more here: emilyorgan.com/penny-green-victorian-mystery-series

The Augusta Peel Series

∾

Meet Augusta Peel, an amateur sleuth with a mysterious past.

She's a middle-aged book repairer who chaperones young ladies and minds other people's pets in her spare time. But there's more to Augusta than meets the eye.

Detective Inspector Fisher of Scotland Yard was well acquainted with Augusta during the war. In 1920s London, no one wishes to discuss those times but he decides Augusta can be relied upon when a tricky murder case comes his way.

Death in Soho is a 1920s cozy mystery set in London in 1921. Featuring actual and fictional locations, the story takes place in colourful Soho and bookish Bloomsbury. A read for fans of page-turning, light mysteries with historical detail!

Find out more here: emilyorgan.com/augusta-peel

Made in the USA
Columbia, SC
17 December 2022

74399106R00102